Angel Trap

Dale Cumberland

Illustrated by Gina Cumberland

iUniverse, Inc.
Bloomington

Angel Trap

iUniverse books may be ordered through booksellers or by contacting:

iUniverse
1663 Liberty Drive
Bloomington, IN 47403
www.iuniverse.com
1-800-Authors (1-800-288-4677)

ISBN: 978-1-4759-5599-6 (sc)
ISBN: 978-1-4759-5600-9 (hc)
ISBN: 978-1-4759-5601-6 (e)

Library of Congress Control Number: 2012919250

Printed in the United States of America

iUniverse rev. date: 10/29/2012

For

Nathan, Mara and Andrew,
without whose inspiration this book
would not have been written.

A special thank you to Dolores Melton
and Yvonne Bays, for editing.

Contents

The Trap

"Do you see one yet?" Mara asked in a hushed voice.

"No — not — yet." In his two years, Aaron had learned enough words to get by on, but he had not been able to put his words together. He talked in long, measured pauses, as if carefully considering his thoughts. Peering intently, Aaron's body froze as his eyes darted back and forth, watching for movement in the shadows. His deep brown eyes met thick, sandy hair, barely peeking out from under his long overdue haircut. Mara, already six, was better at studying her ever observant younger brother for signs of the prey than keeping an eye out for herself. Somehow, Aaron's keen observation never missed a single movement.

Nearby, Ben, nine, the oldest of the three children, let his tousled blond hair lay back in the dust as he watched the late summer clouds aimlessly drift overhead. Finger wrapped tightly with the end of the string, he waited for word that the quarry was nearing the trap. His mind drifted with the clouds but finally settled on the approaching first day of school He wondered what it would be like to ride a school bus for the first time. He decided that he would rather sit in the front of the school bus where he might catch a breeze. The summer had been a hot dry one, without even a hint of rain in weeks. In the distance, he could hear a truck and men laughing down on the bumpy, dusty road that ran past the hunting camp up and on up to the school.

"Here — comes — one!" whispered Aaron, drawing everyone to immediate attention. Ben turned over to his stomach excitedly, his eyes searching for the prey, tensing his body to jerk the string at the right moment. Slowly, the small bird made its way toward the trap, following the trail of sorghum seeds that had been carefully laid on the ground. Seed by seed, the quail pecked toward the wooden box being held up precariously by the forked branch that Ben had so carefully balanced. Ben sat up and held his breath as the bird almost disappeared into the shadow of the box. Cautiously, he took up all slack from the string.

"Now!" yelled Aaron, and Ben jerked on the string as hard as he could, falling over backward as the string flew toward him and tangled at his feet.

"Pull — Now!" shouted Aaron again, thinking that his previous command had been ignored.

"Mara!" Ben hollered, and quickly the brown haired girl stood up, realizing even before Ben called her name that she would bear the brunt of the blame if the quail escaped. She raced toward the box, hoping to retie the knot before the bird could escape. As she passed the end of the slack string, she saw the quail peek out of the box, check out the commotion, and then, with a rush, fly away toward the underbrush.

"Mara!" yelled Ben again, jumping to his feet, "I told you to tie that knot good, and now the only quail we saw all day is flying off." Mara took the end of the string, and hurried to retie the knot to the still erect stick holding the box. Determination covered her small tanned face as she twisted the string around the stick, hoping that this knot would hold against the next pull of her brother.

◆

It had been a slow afternoon at the camp, and with sunset approaching, the hunters returned, anxious to clean the day's six doves and get to the serious business of emptying the cold cans of brew stored in the ice chest. The long drought had left the ground dry and hard baked, and there was little water to attract the birds. Even the pond at the end of the creek had dried, leaving only hard squares of greenish colored clay where the water had once stood. Though disappointed with their meager results, the hunters were still happy to be out at the camp, away from the responsibilities of their jobs.

They drove near the old house that had been abandoned for years, not noticing that this year the windows had fresh drapes and a mowed lawn. They never saw the kids hunched down in the grass under the hackberry tree by the edge of the camp. Loudly, the hunters emerged from the new Ford that had been rigged out for hunting, and tossed the bloody doves up on the porch of the camp. The noise of the hunters unloading their guns flushed a single quail, which, startled by the commotion, had flown down toward the old hackberry tree for safety. With a move trained by instinct, one of the hunters snapped his barrel shut and swung it up high and through the flushing bird. As the bird lowered toward the fence, the hunter fired and cursed, missing his prey for the last time that day.

◆

Ben began to make his way past Aaron, still hollering at Mara when he heard the shot ring out. Freezing, he saw his sister fall in a heap, dust rising as she collapsed on the ground, her foot knocking over the stick holding the box.

"You — got — it!"

"Mara! Oh, Jeez, Mara!" Ben tried to rush to his sister, but froze in his tracks, unable to move. "Mara! Mara!"

"You — got — it!" Aaron cried out again.

Ben suddenly found his feet and rushed toward his sister. "Mara! Mara! Are you shot? Oh, please, God, don't be shot. Mara!" By now Ben was crying, and bending over his sister. He grabbed her and turned her over.

"You — got — it!" screamed an increasingly agitated Aaron. "You — got — it!"

"I'm okay. I must have just tripped over the stick and fell down." Mara, seeing her brother's tears, confused them with anger and tried to soothe his temper. "Don't be mad at me, I was just trying to tie the string again."

"You're not shot? You're okay? Oh, man, thank goodness. Mom would be really mad if you were shot and killed, and it'd be all your fault for not tying that string right anyway." Ben paused, and looked at his sister very hard. "You sure you're not shot?"

"You — got — it! You — got — it! You — got — it!" Aaron's excitement had finally gotten their attention, and they both turned to face him. Aaron was approaching slowly, his arm and finger pointing straight to the box. Turning their gaze from Aaron to the box, they were startled to hear a slight commotion coming from inside.

"You — got — it!" By now, Aaron had reached the box, and gaining Mara's and Ben's attention, had a very satisfactory look on his face.

"We got the bird?" Mara asked both hopeful and astonished.

"All right! Way to go Mara! You did it!" With the look of a conquering warrior, one hand on Mara and the other raised in the air triumphantly Ben shouted, "We did it!"

"No – not – quail, – something – else." Aaron's eyes were big and round, staring intently at the box, which had become very quiet.

Ben and Mara turned to look at the box and then turned back to Aaron. "What else?" Ben asked, searching his brother's eyes for a hint.

"Big – bird!" Aaron replied, still staring at the box.

"How big?" Ben became excited, having never known his brother to make up a story, being too young to lie yet.

"Big! With – wings!"

Ben and Mara both excitedly reached to lift the box, carefully, at the same time. Raising one corner, they peered under the box, lifting it just high enough to not let the bird escape. Aaron stayed back, eyes wide, anticipating seeing the bird that he had just barely glimpsed as the box had come crashing down. The box was quiet as they raised it higher and higher, ever watchful for movement that would indicate imminent escape. Finally, the box was fully lifted. Ben and Mara stood silently, mouths open, too surprised to move.

"I – told – you. You – got – it." Aaron was staring at the open trap, mouth open, moving slowly toward the scene in front of him. The children stood quietly in front of the box, waiting for movement, for sound to come from the creature standing before them.

Aaron was the first to be able to speak. "It – not – bird."

Standing before the three children was the most beautiful little girl that they had ever seen. Aaron was right; she sure wasn't a bird!

Standing upright, she returned the children's gaze with bright blue eyes, unblinking behind thick, dark eyelashes. Her hair, the color of wheat after it had dried in the spring, moved softly in the wind. Her skin was so light colored that the children felt they could almost see right through her. She somehow seemed to be powerful, but at the same time, as frightened and confused as a child. Mara was the first to recover her senses.

"Who are you?' she asked the childlike figure standing in the box, who seemed to be very much her own size.

"My name is Iliana." The words sounded like a musical instrument, something like the combination of a harp and a flute, blowing gently in the wind and yet hovering for moments after they were spoken.

"Do you live around here?" continued Mara, still trying to understand what she was seeing.

"No."

"How did you get in the trap?" Ben asked, finally regaining his senses enough to speak. He still couldn't believe what he was seeing.

"Trap?" Iliana asked, looking at the box that had been lifted over her head. "I don't know. I saw you, Mara, and I was afraid that the bullets would hit you and you would be hurt, so I rushed to push you down. The next thing I remember, I was under that...trap."

Mara looked at Iliana even more confused. "How do you know my name? I didn't see you push me down." Mara's mind was spinning, trying to understand what had happened. "Where did you come from?"

"I don't know, I don't know!" Iliana cried out softly. "I don't think I'm supposed to be here, and I think I should go back."

Ben saw tears gathering on Iliana's cheeks, and she appeared more confused than ever. She seemed unable to answer the questions, and glanced around as if she were looking for help. "I'm sorry that we trapped you," Ben spoke apologetically. "We were just trying to catch a bird, and the trap must have fallen on you by mistake. I don't know where you came from, but I think we ought to go see our mom. She'll know what to do, and she'll help you get back home."

Mara and Ben each took one of Iliana's hands, and began to lead her back to the old farmhouse, with Aaron following closely behind. They couldn't quite understand what Aaron was saying behind them as they made their way, watching Iliana's every step.

"No – catch – bird, – catch – angel. No – catch – bird, – catch – angel." Aaron muttered, over and over to himself.

Micah

Micah was standing at the kitchen sink, finishing the supper dishes, watching for her children's return from playing down by the shade tree. She neatly stacked the plates behind the glass doors in the kitchen cupboard, closing the doors carefully so the panes with the missing glazing would not fall out. The old farmhouse next to the hunting camp had been vacant for years, and the paint had begun to curl on the wood siding, needing to be scraped and repainted. Micah reached up, adjusting her thick brown hair caught up in a pony tail. She had worried about her children moving to the old house, hoping that the adjustment to the new school would be somewhat easy. They had all been very comfortable in their big, new home at the edge of the town where they had moved from, just a short walk from Mara's school. She missed her home, and prayed that the children didn't become angry from having to leave all of the things that they had loved in their previous home. If only their father hadn't...

The children returning from play suddenly caught her attention, and her thoughts focused on the image approaching her. Where in the world had her children found a friend way out here? Something about their gait made her worry, and she sensed that her children were anxious. Maybe it was just about their new acquaintance.

"Mom. Mom!"

She laid her cup towel down and moved to the screen door and out on to the back porch. Carefully, she stepped over the rotting second step, and walked to meet the approaching group.

"Mom! You're not going to believe this!" shouted Ben. "We found someone, and I think she's lost, and you have to help her get home!"

"We – caught – a – angel!" Aaron was churning his small short legs as fast as he could, running ahead of his brother and sister, anxious to be the first to tell the news.

"Well, who do we have here? My, you sure are a pretty thing." Micah thought to herself that she had never seen such a beautiful child, and was astounded that she had wandered out to the isolated farmhouse. Her eyes fell to the young girl's dress, a beautiful silvery white gown that fell almost to her feet. She wondered how the child could keep her dress so clean, out here with all of the dust, and she wished to herself that she would be able to keep her own children so neat and clean looking. "Come on in, and let's give your parents a call." The children and their new friend were up on the porch. "Don't you worry about anything, honey. Everything is going to be all right."

Micah bent down to comfort her children's friend, and for the first time, got a good look at her face. The little girl was extraordinary — and those eyes. It was as though Micah could see herself in their depths.

"You okay? Let's get you inside. Are you hungry? Have you had anything to eat? What's your name, honey?"

"My name is Iliana." The voice replied so softly, so sweetly.

"Iliana, where are you from?"

"I don't think I'm from around here." Iliana seemed confused as she gazed into Micah's eyes.

"Well, are you visiting someone around here? Up at the hunting camp maybe?"

"No." Iliana paused and squinted her eyes as though she was trying to remember. "I was just watching Mara. I was trying to protect her."

"Protect her! Mara needs some protecting all right, but I don't know if you're the right one to do that! Come on in, and let's get you something to eat while I figure out how to get hold of your mom and dad." Micah wondered what Iliana had meant by protecting Mara, but brushed it aside in order to get to the business of finding the young girl's parents.

The three children and their new friend came through the back door and settled around the kitchen table. Unlike the house, the table was sturdy, but set unevenly on the rolling linoleum floor. Micah took four glasses from the cupboard, filled them with fresh lemonade, set them before the children, and searched the pantry for the cookies she had put away for the first day of school. Opening the fresh pack of cookies, she counted out two for each of the children.

"Gingerbread Man cookies! I love Gingerbread Man cookies!" Mara picked up her two cookies and set them before her neatly, laughingly anticipating the sweet, spicy treat. Aaron picked up his two cookies and began a conversation between the two of them, while Ben excitedly chomped off the head of the first cookie, wondering what part of its body the decapitated man would sacrifice to his taste buds next.

Iliana stared quietly at her cookies, as though she was unsure about what to do with them. Finally, sensing the joy of the children eating the cookies, she took a small taste of the Gingerbread Man, nibbling gently on his foot. "Mmmm, this is very good!" Iliana smiled and seemed totally absorbed in the taste of the gingerbread.

"Why, thank you, Iliana. Gingerbread's one of my favorites, too." Micah smiled at Iliana, drawn to the small girl's enthusiasm for the cookie. She reached over instinctively to brush Iliana's golden hair from her face, and tucked a lock gently behind her ear. "Iliana, where do live? I bet your parents are worried about you. Let's give them a call."

"I don't know," said Iliana softly, turning her head as if trying to remember. Her answer seemed genuine, as did her confusion about the question.

"Well, that's okay, Iliana. Lots of kids your age don't know where they live. We just moved here ourselves, and I bet Mara hasn't learned her new address yet either." Micah smiled at Mara, and wondered if she was right. Mara looked up from her cookies and smiled, not admitting if her mom was right or not.

"I know!" shouted Ben. "Route 1, Box 28 on Farm Road 119 in Hondo, Texas!" Ben plopped the headless, armless, legless body of his last Gingerbread Man into his mouth, and grinned proudly. Micah smiled at him approvingly and turned her attention back to Iliana.

"What's your last name? We'll give your mom and dad a call. They'll be glad to know you're here, all safe and everything."

"Last name?" Iliana seemed confused. "I don't think I have a last name; I'm only Iliana."

"Everyone has a last name, Iliana. Ben and Mara and Aaron's last name is Summers. Your mom and dad have last name, like 'Mr. Applebutter' or 'Mrs. Figwhite.'" Mara and Aaron giggled at hearing the names their mom had read from the story at bedtime last night. Micah wondered if Iliana lived with both her mom and dad, or … "Iliana," Micah asked softly, "Do you live with your mom, or with your dad…" Searching Iliana's eyes, and seeing no response, Micah continued, "or with someone else?"

Iliana looked confused, but seemed glad to be able to give an answer. "I live with someone else." She smiled happily, and hoped that the information was enough to please her host.

Micah gazed at Iliana, and her mind drifted to her own children, and how they missed their own dad, and what it would be like to miss both parents. She was reluctant to press on with her questions for fear of upsetting the beautiful child, but she knew that she had to get to the bottom of this mystery.

"Who else? Your grandparents, an aunt and uncle?" Micah searched her own mind for the possible whereabouts of the girl's family. All that she found, though, was Iliana's own searching eyes staring back, looking deeply into her eyes for a clue of her own.

"She — from — heaven. She — a — angel!" Aaron had finished his last gingerbread man cookies, and had decided to help out. "She — got — wings!"

"Oh my gosh, Aaron, what a good imagination! She sure looks like an angel…" Micah paused and turned to Iliana, and after giving fancy to Aaron's words, shook her head, and finished her sentence directed at Iliana "but I think you're from a whole lot closer to Hondo than you are from heaven."

Micah stood stretching her long, slender legs. She picked up the cup towel from the sink and began to wipe the cookie crumbs from the table. She considered that maybe Iliana wasn't quite ready, for whatever reason, to cooperate in Micah's search for her home. Maybe she had run away, maybe for good reason. Micah decided to try to let her relax and play with the kids for awhile, and maybe gain her confidence in time. "I tell you what. Why don't you kids run upstairs and take a bath? Ben and Mara, you've got a big day tomorrow starting a brand new school and all, and I want you going to bed right after your bath. I'll be up to tuck you in and say prayers as soon as I finish cleaning up down here. Mara, pick out some of your good clothes for Iliana to change into after her bath, and Aaron, don't be splashing water on the floor — that ceiling is just about to come down under the bathroom already!"

Micah watched as the four children jumped up from the table and scampered up the stairs, with Aaron trying his best to keep up with Ben, and Mara carefully leading Iliana up the loud wooden treads. She smiled thankfully that her three children were home with her tonight, and not out lost. She hoped that she would be able to find Iliana's family by that evening.

◆

"Come on, Iliana, you can bathe with me." Mara watched as Ben and Aaron tumbled into the only bathroom, and heard the water creak through the old pipes. Mara had never thought it fair that Ben and Aaron could bathe together and she had to bathe alone. They always sounded like they had so much fun splashing and giggling in the tub. "Let's pick out some night clothes for you to wear."

Iliana looked in wonderment as Mara opened the drawers of her oak chest. Mara picked a pair of underpants from the neatly stacked pile in the top drawer, and then chose a soft cotton pink gown from the second drawer and handed then to Iliana. "This is my favorite nightgown, but I want you to wear it. You'll look pretty in pink. And here is a pink clip for your hair, I always wear it when I go to bed, but you can wear it tonight." Mara looked at Iliana and smiled, glad to have a friend to share with. Iliana was the first friend that she had met since moving to the farmhouse, and she was thankful.

"I hope Mom finds your mom and dad tonight, but if she doesn't, you can sleep with me!" Iliana smiled brightly at Mara. She didn't say much, but her smile spoke to Mara's heart. "Do you want to sleep with me in my bed?" asked Mara, beginning to hope that her mom would be unsuccessful in her search.

"I would like that!" Iliana smiled again and looked around the room. The large dresser and the canopied bed were the only furniture in the room. Mara's mom had hung pink and white curtains in the window, and a gentle summer breeze was slowly blowing them into the room. Bright pictures of kittens and angels lined the whitewashed wooden walls, giving the room a cheery look even in the light of the single bulb hanging from the ceiling. Iliana thought that she would like to spend the night with Mara very much.

The bathroom door flew open, and Aaron scurried out with a towel wrapped around his waist. "Hurry, Aaron, or I'll eat you!" Ben cried out in a deep voice, emerging from the bathroom with his arms raised high, walking with long, monster steps after his little brother.

"No – not – eat – me!" giggled Aaron back, and both boys raced into the bedroom at the end of the hall. Iliana watched as the door closed, and then turned back to Mara and giggled.

Mara and Iliana took their turns in the bath, and after dressing in the soft cotton nightgowns, crawled into the single bed and shared a pillow. The boys had settled down to a quiet murmur in the bedroom at the end of the hall, and the evening quiet was beginning to take hold of the farmhouse. Micah's light steps coming up the stairs comforted the children, reminding them that they were not alone in the old house. The girls listened as they heard the sound of the steps lead down to the end bedroom, and after hearing muffled voices, heard a scurry of steps come back down the hall to Mara's room. Aaron entered first, wearing a long nightshirt with a kangaroo on it, and pounced on the girl's bed. "Mom – gonna – tell – story!" Ben followed Micah into the room, and they both sat on the end of the bed.

Micah smiled at the two girls snuggled now with Aaron. "How was yall's bath? Did you shampoo Iliana's hair?" The strawberry fragrance of freshly washed hair filled the air of the bedroom.

"Yep, shampooed and conditioned," Mara reported happily. "And all brushed out, too!"

Iliana smiled softly at Micah from the pillow. She seemed to glow in her comfort, and Micah wondered if she missed her own bed. She decided to put off her questions until a little later.

"Well, tonight, since we have a special visitor, I brought Aaron and Ben in here to tell you a bed time story." Aaron snuggled in warmly between the two girls. Ben leaned back against the wall, and tried to avoid the feet of his sister, who pulled them up under her knees.

"Once upon a time, a long time ago," Micah began, starting her stories as she always did, "There was a beautiful girl with long golden hair named Goldilocks."

Ben groaned under his breath, having hoped for a new story, and slouched a little more deeply onto the foot of the bed. Micah turned to him, and gave him a quick glance of warning with a smile before continuing. "And she was lost in the woods. After wandering around for hours, she stumbled into a little house in the woods where a bear family had just gone for a walk before eating their supper porridge."

Aaron listened wide eyed to the familiar story about the three bears, giggling as his mom made the deep imitation of Papa Bear's voice. Mara and Iliana lay attentively, smiling with each anticipated turn in the story. Ben heeded his mother's warning and sat quietly until joining in a chorus with the other children when Micah had finished the story "The end!"

"I like that story, Mom. Tell us another one, please?" wheedled Mara, hoping for her mother to continue. Micah took hold of her small hand, and with a shake of her head, replied, "Not tonight — we have other things to talk about."

Micah turned to Iliana and thought how comfortable and happy she appeared, lying under the blankets with Mara and Aaron. She hoped that this would not be the last evening that her children could spend with Iliana, that they would all become good friends. She wondered if Iliana was ready to open up to her.

"Iliana, I still need to get a hold of your family," Micah began, and breathed a short sigh before continuing. "Do you remember your last name yet?" Micah searched Iliana's eyes, and hoped for the child's family's sake that this would be easy. Iliana stared back, and slowly shook her head with out showing any expression on her face.

Micah considered what approach to try next, and after a short pause, she decided to backtrack. "Okay, let's start at the beginning. Ben, where did you first see Iliana?" Ben seemed surprised at the question, and in the excitement of bringing Iliana home, realized that he had forgotten to tell how Iliana had first appeared.

"We, um, caught her in a trap," Ben began, beginning to doubt the credibility of his story. Glancing at Mara, Aaron, and Iliana, he continued cautiously. "We were playing down by the hackberry tree, trying to catch a quail with an old wood box we found. I saw a quail go under the box."

"I — saw — quail — go — under — box!" Aaron interrupted briefly but emphatically.

After catching a quick breath, Ben continued, thinking to himself that he would have to be very precise in his story, or continue to be interrupted. "Anyways, I pulled the string, and Mara had tied it all wrong or something, so it came loose from the stick, so I hollered for Mara to go fix it. It was the only quail we saw all afternoon, and Mara had let it get away." Ben glanced at his sister, wondering if he would be challenged. He paused, remembering the gun shot and his sister laying on the ground, and quickly decided that was not information that his mom needed, as he had been warned about playing too close to the hunting camp on several occasions. Then remembering his sister on the ground again, he quickly added, "Well, it probably wasn't her fault anyway. I might have jerked it too hard." He winced at seeing the satisfaction on his sister's face, but decided that he was choosing the only safe explanation. "Anyways, the box fell over, and when we lifted it, Iliana was in it!" Ben shrugged his shoulders, and looked at his Micah's face, and then down to the throw rug at the foot of the bed. Taking a deep breath, he looked back at his mom's face, trying to interpret her expression.

"You found Iliana in the box?" Micah asked incredulously. She looked at Ben, and then at Mara, cocking her head slightly while waiting for a better explanation.

Mara looked at her mom, looked back at Ben, and then to her mom again. She offered no further explanation and scooted closer to Iliana under the covers.

"She — was — a — angel! 'Liana — had — wings!" Aaron was sticking to his story. He returned his mom's grin, and pulled the covers up slightly over his head.

Micah shook her head, and still smiling, turned towards Iliana. "Iliana, honey, did they find you in a box?"

"Yes ma'am." Iliana spoke brightly and cheerfully, but offered nothing more than affirmation of Ben's story.

"Well, okay." Micah continued, "How did you get into the box?"

Iliana smiled again before answering "It fell on top of me?" The other children began to giggle as they surveyed the looks on their mom's face. Micah's eyes were wide, and her mouth was slightly open. She was leaning over in anticipation of the full explanation, hoping to draw the story out from Iliana, but unable to get anything but simple answers.

"Okay, Iliana," Micah sang, beginning to play along with the child's answers, turning the debriefing into a game. "How did the box fall on top of you?"

"Mara knocked it over!" Iliana said, laughing along with the other children.

"And how did Mara knock it over?" Micah asked with a mock stern look on her face.

"I tripped over the stick!" Mara offered, and all of the children broke into open laughter watching Micah's face contort with mock exasperation. Micah then broke into laughter with the children, and reached down and gave one big hug to Mara, Aaron, and Iliana in the blankets, giving them all soft tickles as they squirmed under her arms. She sat back up on the edge of the bed and waited for the children to quiet.

"Okay, okay. Let's get serious." Micah regrouped, and directed her attention once again to Iliana. "Iliana, how did you get here, to where the kids were playing. Where did you come from?" The children realized that Micah's tone had changed, and the giggling disappeared as they all turned attentively to Iliana, wondering what the answer was. Iliana stared back quietly at Micah, and slowly shaking her head, answered softly "I don't know." Moments passed, and Iliana realized that as it continued, she would have to give a more complete explanation. She closed her eyes, as if concentrating very hard, and shaking her head very slightly, offered slowly, "I was watching Mara, and when I saw that she was in trouble, I just rushed to protect her. That's when the box fell on top of me. It was very dark, and then the box lifted, and I saw Mara, and Ben, and Aaron." Iliana looked at each of the children and smiled as she said their names.

Micah continued to gaze at Iliana, wondering where the story was leading, but determined to follow every possible lead. "Mara was in trouble? What kind of trouble was she in, Iliana? What was she doing?"

Ben looked quickly from Micah to Iliana, wondering how she would complete her story.

Iliana looked at Mara, and smiling, continued the explanation. "Mara was getting ready to tie the string to the trap, and one of the hunters shot at a bird, but he missed. The shot was coming straight toward Mara, and I wanted to protect her from being hurt, so I pushed her down." Turning to face an incredulous looking Micah, she finished, "When Mara fell down, she knocked over the box and I was trapped inside."

This new information, given so completely, stunned Micah, and caused her to pause. Looking at Iliana, a dozen questions jumped to her consciousness, and she tried to sort through them. The pause gave Ben an opportunity to try for redemption as he realized that Iliana's sudden illumination had exposed certain truths that he had tried to gloss over.

"Mom, I know we aren't supposed to be down by the camp, but it's the only place where the quail come so we can trap 'em." Ben looked at his sister, and remembering her lying on the ground, sighed and came out with more truth than he had intended. "I heard a shot come from the camp, and I saw Mara fall down. I thought she got shot. She was just lying there on the ground, not moving. I didn't want her to be hurt – I rushed down to her to see if she was ok." Thinking back, he remembered his elation on discovering that his sister was in fact not injured. "She didn't get hurt even one little bit. And then Aaron hollered out that we had caught a quail."

"A – angel!" Aaron again interrupted.

Ben, paused, and then continued, "Anywise, we opened the trap, and there she was!"

Micah was beginning to get frustrated at her attempts to find Iliana's origin. The questioning had produced information, some of which Micah decided to deal with later on, but none of which was leading to how to get Iliana home. She looked at her children, and then at Iliana, and whispered a short prayer to herself, "O lord..."

"Iliana, we need to get you home. Can you help us? I just need to know where you live, where you came from. I need to call your family — I need to know your phone number, or your last name, or the name of a relative, or a friend. Just something, anything that can help us. Iliana, can you help?" Micah sat quietly, hoping, praying that Iliana could give her the information that she needed.

Iliana sat quietly, and then, after several moments, she smiled softly. "I only know that my name is Iliana, and I don't know the names of any relatives. I wish I could tell you where I came from, but I can't. I'm sorry, Mara's Mom, but I don't know what to tell you." Micah smiled back at Iliana, and touched by the name, said quietly, "My name is Micah Summers. Iliana, if you want, you can call me Mom."

Micah sat quietly for a moment, and then decided that, for tonight, her task was finished. Whatever mystery Iliana kept would have to wait for morning. "Iliana, why don't you sleep with Mara tonight. We'll find your family tomorrow." Micah watched as Iliana smiled at her and felt comforted that she had made the right decision.

"Ben, Aaron, let's all say our prayers together before I put you in bed. Ben, you start tonight." Ben slid to his knees at the foot of the bed, and made a quick motion to his forehead. "In the name of the Father..." Micah listened quietly as Ben led the other children in their night prayers. "God bless Mommy, God bless Daddy..." Ben continued with the long litany of "God blesses" that included family members and friends, old and new. "...God bless Iliana..." Micah glanced up and smiled at Iliana, and saw her sitting up in bed, eyes closed, hands clasped.

The prayers continued with the "Our Father," a "Hail Mary" led by Mara, and an attempt at the "Glory Be" by Aaron, that had to be finished by Micah as Aaron could still not get past "to – the – Father…" Finally, the children joined in the final chorus that kept them safe through the night:

"Angel of God, my guardian dear,

To whom His love entrusts me here,

Ever this night be at my side,

To light and guard, To rule and guide.

Amen."

Ben stood and gave Micah a hug as Aaron crawled out from between Iliana and Mara. "I love you Mom, good night."

"I – love – you – Mom – good – night," echoed Aaron, as he received Micah's kiss on the forehead. Ben picked up his younger brother and carried him off to bed while Aaron began to giggle once again. Micah issued a warning as they headed down the hall, "Ben, you boys go right to sleep – tomorrow's a big day. Aaron, you go right to sleep!" The sound of both boys giggling disappeared into the room at the end of the hall.

"I love you, Mom." Mara stood in the bed just long enough to give Micah a hug, and then dropped back under the covers. Iliana hesitated as if uncertain as to what to do, and then jumped up and gave Micah a hug "I love you, Mara's Mom. Goodnight!"

◆

Mara listened as Micah's footsteps disappeared down the hall into the middle room. She felt the darkness cover her as light from Micah's bedroom faded with the closing of her door. She felt safe in her bed as she inched closer to Iliana, watching as the moonlight streaming in the bedroom window grew brighter as her eyes accustomed to the soothing darkness. "Iliana," she asked, "were you watching me down under the hackberry tree?"

Mara felt Iliana roll to her back as if awakening. "Yes," she answered. And then, offering more, said, "Mara, I have always watched you."

Mara lay quietly, thinking about what Iliana had said. "Always?" She asked, not sure she understood.

"Yes, always. Since you were a baby, since before you were born, I have been with you, watching you. Hoping for you. Praying for you."

Mara felt uncertain, and yawning, asked "You were watching me? I never saw you."

"I was always there with you."

"Were you invisible?" asked Mara, becoming more sleepy, trying to understand.

"You couldn't see me, but I was always there. I was with you today when you were under the hackberry tree."

"I didn't see you, Iliana. But I'm glad you were there." Mara reached over and held Iliana's hand. She felt happy knowing that Iliana was with her. She lay quietly, and her eyes began to close, blinking longer and longer.

"Mara?" Mara heard the voice almost as in a dream. "Mara? Why did you catch me in that box under the tree?" The voice continued, almost in a whisper, and seemed to disappear into the darkness. "Mara, I am afraid." Finally, the blinks became one long blink that did not open, and quiet filled the home.

The Sheriff

Aaron rolled over and put his feet quietly on the floor. Looking at Ben still covered under the sheets, he realized that he was the first to awake. He walked to the window, and seeing the eastern sky filling with light was satisfied that it was indeed morning, and that he would be received in other quarters. He steadfastly made his way down the hall to the first door and opened it carefully. Tiptoeing to the side of the bed, he carefully pulled himself up and swung his leg high over the oak railing on the bottom of the bed. He silently crawled under the sheet next to the sleeping body and lay still, thinking about his next move. From below, he heard a rooster crow, and as if on signal, sat up in bed and spoke. "Cereal. I – want – cereal." Patiently, he waited for a response. Moments passed as he considered his options. Then another rooster crow set off another request. "Please – Mom. I – want – cereal." The body next to his responded and gently rolled over to begin the day.

◆

"Ben, hurry down or you'll be late." The breakfast table was already filled with three young bodies and three boxes of cereal. Aaron sat hunched over his now empty bowl, protecting the box of Cocoa Pebbles, studying the puzzle on the back and stirring his empty, brown milk. He seemed annoyed that others had invaded his familiar summer solitude of breakfast alone with his mom. Mara and Iliana were sharing the box of Frosty Alphabets, trying to find the necessary letters to finish their names.

"Coming, Mom!" The voice barely beat the rushing feet down the stairs as Ben appeared wearing khaki pants and a new Polo shirt. His Nikes were tired and worn, but the new shoestrings gave them an appearance of fashion that he hoped would meet the minimal requirements for the fourth grade. His dark blonde hair was still wet and combed straight back. He headed for the pantry and looked for the new box of Lucky Charms that he had seen his mom buy for the special occasion.

"They're on the table!" Micah yelled over the noise, sensing what Ben was searching for. Ben turned and took his chair at the table. He filled his bowl, covered the cereal with milk, and added a spoonful of sugar after making sure Micah wasn't watching.

"You – goin' – to – school?" Aaron looked up from his brown milk to watch his brother dig into the bowl. With his mouth full, Ben could only nod vigorously.

"You – goin' – to – ride – school – bus?"

Ben swallowed, excitedly answered, 'Yeah', and crammed another spoonful in his mouth.

"I – goin' – to – ride – yellow – school – bus, – too!" Aaron looked up hopefully, wishing to not be challenged in his desire.

"No, Aaron, not this year. You're almost three, and you have to wait two more years to ride to school." Micah saw the disappointment in Aaron's eyes and made a promise. "Today, just you and me will take a ride to town. Okay?"

Aaron, still looking disappointed, looked up and said "O – kay" and returned to stirring his cereal.

"Mom, can Iliana please ride the school bus with me?" Mara was pleading what seemed to be a lost cause.

"No, Mara. I already told you, Iliana has to stay here while we figure out where her folks live." Mara and Iliana already seemed inseparable, and Micah wanted to say yes but knew that she had to contact Iliana's family as soon as possible. Surely they must be worried to death by now. She wondered if the two girls would ever see each other again after Mara got on the bus. She thought about explaining that probable outcome to Mara to ease her disappointment but decided not to add anxiety to the stress of her first day at a new school. "Come on and finish your cereal, and we'll walk down to the mailbox so you can catch the bus. We don't wanna be late the first day!"

Ben finished gulping the last of the milk from his bowl just in time to hear the phone ring. "I'll get it!" he yelled, as he made his way across the crowded kitchen to the living room to answer the phone. Micah watched, guessing the nature of the early morning call.

"Mom, it's the sheriff! He says he wants to talk to you!" Ben hollered back into the dining room. "Hurry!"

"The – sheriff?" asked Aaron, and all activity stopped at the breakfast table as three sets of eyes watched Micah wipe her hands on her apron and make her way to answer the phone. The children listened as she said 'Hello?', and strained to hear as Micah turned her back to the children and talked in a quiet, hushed voice. She stood there, leaning against the back of the couch nervously scratching the back of her head, and turned only once, glancing briefly at Iliana. Finally, she hung up the phone and stood with her back still to the children for a few moments before turning around with a practiced smile on her face.

"Okay, kiddos, lets' get down to the mailbox before we miss the bus. Ben! Mara! Grab your lunch sacks from the refrigerator, and don't forget your backpacks by the back door. Scoot; let's go before it's too late. Come on, Iliana, you can walk with me and Aaron to see the kids get on the bus. Hurry!" Micah ushered orders into the swarming chaos as children rushed around gathering up last minute items, remembering school and forgetting about the phone call.

Aaron jumped up and was the first to reach the door. "I – beat – you!" he offered to any takers. Ben raced to meet the challenge, almost knocking Aaron over as he raced ahead down the dirt road to the mailbox. "Come – on!" Aaron yelled back to Mara and Iliana, who were emptying their bowls in the kitchen sink.

Mara picked up her lunch and took a peek inside. Seeing two Oreo cookies wrapped carefully and sitting on top of a shiny apple, Mara looked up at her mom and smiled. "Thanks!" and pleaded one last time, asked "You sure Iliana can't come with me?"

Micah smiled, and feigning exasperation, took Mara squarely by the shoulders and said with exaggerated loudness, "No! Now get on down to the mailbox before you miss that bus!"

"Okay." Mara smiled back and took Iliana by the hand. The two girls made their way out the door and headed toward the bus stop, laughing and giggling as they went. Micah put down her dishtowel, looking around one last time for anything left behind and followed the four children.

By the time Micah arrived at the mailbox, Ben had already climbed as high into the pear tree that grew at the end of the road as the frail limbs would allow. He watched intently toward the west, past the hunting camp, for signs of the approaching bus.

"Do – you – see – it?" Aaron stood under the tree in his overalls, looking up in the branches at his older brother. "Is – it – coming?" Mara and Iliana stood by the culvert running under the road, picking the late summer flowers that had come up in spite of the lingering drought. Micah loved the smell of the early morning dew and the way that it contained the dust, keeping it from blowing and kicking up under the children's feet. She looked carefully at Ben and Mara, hoping that they would be able to stay clean at least until they got onto the bus.

"It's coming!" Ben yelled out, keeping his perch in the tree. Out to the west, Micah could make out the bus's dust trail that even the dew could not hold down. Mara and Iliana looked up and began to gather the flowers into Mara's backpack. Shoving his chubby hands into his pockets, Aaron strained to see the bright yellow bus.

The sound of the bus shifting gears up the hill was soon followed by the bright yellow top above the low trees that led to the hunting camp. The excitement brought Ben down in a hurry as he rushed to stand close to the mailbox, ensuring a spot that would position himself in front of his sister. Aaron followed his brother closely, trying to imitate his posture, looking up at Ben and then to the approaching bus, still hoping to get a ride on the big bus.

Mara finished putting all but two of the pale blue flowers into her backpack, and taking one flower, turned to her new friend. "Iliana, I saved this one for you. It's the prettiest one." Mara offered the flower gently to Iliana and added thoughtfully, "In case I don't see you again."

The girls stood silently, looking at one another, expressing their feelings with only their eyes, until Iliana stepped forward to give Mara a hug. "Thank you, Mara. It's beautiful! But don't worry, I promise to be here when you get back. I'll be waiting right here by the mailbox for you." Iliana stepped back as the roar of the school bus slowed in front of Ben and Aaron, and smiled again at Mara.

Mara smiled back and rushed to her mom. "Here, Mom. I love you!" she said, as she handed the last flower to her mom and jumped in line behind her brothers.

The bus stopped with a loud squeal of the brakes and a hiss as the door opened. Ben jumped excitedly up the steps and disappeared into the seats, as Aaron tried to negotiate the first step. The bus driver smiled as Micah lifted him carefully up into the bus. "See, Aaron? A school bus! It's going to take Ben and Mara to school. When you get older, you can ride, too!" Hoping that the quick peek would satisfy her youngest child, Micah pulled the excited Aaron off the bus.

"Wow! A – big – school – bus!" Aaron pronounced, happy to have been able to look inside the giant yellow bus.

Mara slowly took the first step after her mom had removed Aaron and tentatively began the climb up the three stairs. At the top, she answered the 'Good morning' of the attractive lady bus driver, and turned to face her mom, Aaron and Iliana one last time. "Bye, Mom! Bye Aaron! Bye, Iliana! See you after school!" Mara yelled out bravely, and followed Ben into the back of the bus. Moments later, the door again hissed closed, and slowly began to pull away. Micah, Aaron and Iliana were happy to spot Mara and Ben through the windows of the bus, and gave them a final wave goodbye as the bus slowly continued east towards Hondo.

Deep inside the bus, Mara felt a cold and empty feeling, as though alone for the first time in her life. She sighed, trying to fight off the fear that crept into her as the bus made its way toward her new school. She began to wish that she had not begged her mom to let her ride the bus the first day, and was instead riding in the car with her mom and Iliana. She looked back, hoping to catch a final glimpse of the waving figures at the mailbox.

"Wow! A – big – school – bus!" Aaron repeated, digging his hands into his overalls as he watched the bus disappear into the still rising sun. Micah retrieved his hand and placed it firmly in her own, turning him back toward the house. As she reached for Iliana's hand, she worried about the tears inching down young girl cheeks as the bus faded out of sight.

"Iliana, you okay?" she asked, as the three made their way back to the house. She wondered what the child was thinking and watched her face for clues. She suspected that Iliana was beginning to miss her own family.

Iliana turned to Micah, and wiping her cheeks with the back of her hand, smiled at Micah's searching eyes. "I'm okay. I'm just gonna miss Mara. I hope that she'll be all right." Iliana sighed and let the smile disappear from her face as she turned forward to face the approaching house. Micah continued watching her as they continued down the trail, wondering more and more about this fragile young girl.

◆

"A – nother – one – Mom!" Aaron excitedly placed the egg in the growing basket, admiring its shape and color. Gathering the eggs was his favorite morning activity since moving to the farm house. Though Micah missed the comfortable home that she and the children had been forced to leave, moments like this made her glad that they were here. She looked with admiration at the repairs Ben had made to the abandoned chicken pen, at his ingenuity at using some of the discarded materials around the house to patch the holes in the rusted tin and wire structure. The children had adjusted to 'life on the farm' much easier than she had hoped. They had learned to match their own pace with the daily farm activities.

Micah was glad that she had overcome her hesitation at accepting the chickens from Mr. Hawkins down the road, who had insisted that every good farm had to have at least a few chickens running around. She had grown fond of the birds, and enjoyed their clucking and early morning wake up calls. Even the eggs tasted better than the ones she used to buy, though she had a difficult time convincing herself to eat the first one. "Look, Mom, the poop washes right off!" she remembered Mara's happy exclamation at the kitchen sink, and laughed to herself as she recalled her disgust. She shook her head at the recollection, trying to again convince herself that the eggs were safe to eat.

"Sorry – Mom. I – broke – one." Aaron's face was twisted into a frown as he looked at the dripping clear and yellow goo coming from his hand. The sight brought her quickly back to real time as she tried to find something safe on which the young boy could wipe his hands. ""It's – o – kay." Aaron responded to his mom's search by reaching down and wiping his hand on the front of his overalls, and looking up at his mom and grinning at her dismay. "I – clean – it!"

"Here, Mara's Mom, here's the tissue you gave me earlier," offered Iliana belatedly. She stood back, holding out her arm, trying to avoid the growing mess. "You can use it if you want to."

Micah was reaching out for the tissue when she saw the approaching car from over Iliana's shoulder. Though not entirely visible, she could easily make out the rectangular plastic red and white lights on top of the car. "He's here already," she gasped slightly as she hurriedly wiped the egg from Aaron's overalls. "Come on, kids, let's go take the eggs to the house. We've got company!" Micah tried to cover her anxiety with a smile, and held open the door to the chicken coop, waiting for Iliana and Aaron to exit.

The sheriff was already knocking at the front door by the time Micah and the children came into the kitchen. "Iliana, honey, would you mind helping Aaron with those eggs?" she asked, as she picked up a dishcloth to wipe her hands, and headed towards the door. Walking across the living room, she began to wonder if she had done the right thing.

"Hello, Sheriff, come on in!" Micah smiled brightly at the large figure that towered in her door. Bending down so as not to bump his well worn Stetson hat on the door casing, the sheriff entered and looked around.

"Good morning, Mrs. Summers. I came out as quick as I could." The sheriff removed his hat, and smiled at Micah, an open, friendly smile that seemed genuine. His red face looked at her kindly over his double chin, and he looked around for a place to sit his frame. He seemed to be uncomfortable as he stood, shifting his weight from foot to foot. Looking up, he asked, "Is this the little girl you called about?"

Micah turned to follow the sheriff's gaze to see Iliana standing in the kitchen doorway, with Aaron peeking from behind her, still wiping his hands on his overalls. "Iliana, come on in. There's someone here I want you to meet." Iliana smiled cautiously, and approached Micah. Aaron followed closely behind, hiding behind Iliana and peeking out from around her shoulder. Micah pulled Iliana close to herself, put her arm around her shoulder and smiled at her. "Yes, Sheriff, this here is Iliana." Micah smiled at the sheriff, and reached out with her other arm to pull Aaron in close beside her.

"Well, hello, little lady! My, aren't you a purty thing. Isn't she a purty thing, Mrs. Summers?" The sheriff had pulled a red bandana from his back pocket and was wiping his forehead. He glanced around again for a place to sit his large frame down and spied the overstuffed red recliner sitting next to the couch. Looking back at Micah, he asked, "Is it okay if I sit down over there?"

"Sure, Sheriff. Make yourself comfortable." Though Micah had met the sheriff briefly when she had first moved out to the house, she still did not feel comfortable with the imposing figure. "Iliana, Aaron, you go sit on the couch. Sheriff, can I get you something to drink?" Micah asked, wondering if she had anything other than water or milk to offer.

"Sure, I'll take a glass of water, if you have it. Thank you, Mrs. Summers." The sheriff settled into the recliner and carefully rocked back, testing his weight against the chair's springs. Micah watched apprehensively as the two children sat down on the couch at the far end, away from the sheriff, then hurried to get the water and return.

"So, Anna, where you from?" The sheriff leaned forward in the recliner and looked directly at Iliana, raising his eyebrows until they formed deep furrows on his forehead.

"My name is Iliana." Iliana said her name carefully and slowly for the sheriff and smiled at him brightly but offered no other information.

"You live around here?" the sheriff continued, ignoring Iliana's comment. His expression remained unchanged as he slowly moved his large, heavy hands around the brim of his hat.

"I live here, now." Iliana smiled again, and raised her own eyebrows to match those of the sheriff.

"Well, you gotta have family around here somewhere. I ain't never seen you around before," the sheriff paused, looking Iliana over carefully, and then continued, "but your folks has got to be worried by now. What's your last name, Anna?"

Iliana smiled more intently, "My name is Iliana."

"I know that, honey, but what's your last name? Your last name, now, hear me? Go on!" the sheriff's expression remained unchanged, but he leaned slightly back in the chair.

"My name is just Iliana, sir. I don't think I have a last name. I'm sorry," Iliana apologized, and seemed to be sincere.

"Oh come on, Anna, everyone's got to have a last name. Just tell me what it is, and I'll take you right back to your folks. No one's gonna be mad, they're just gonna be glad to have you back. Now, think about it, and tell me who you are." The sheriff leaned as close to Iliana as the recliner would allow, trying to intimidate the small figure into telling the truth. He sat expectantly, breathing loudly through his nose.

Iliana closed her eyes as if concentrating. She opened them, sighed, and spoke slowly, "I'm really sorry, but I think that Iliana is the only name I have. I wish I had a last name, then I could tell you, but I'm certain that is my only name." Iliana sunk back into the couch, her eyes beginning to cloud over. She looked up to see Micah returning with a tray with four glasses of water, and smiled.

The sheriff leaned back away from Iliana when he saw Micah entering the room. Aaron realized the pause in the interrogation, and decided to volunteer his information. "Liana's – a – angel! She – got – wings!"

The sheriff briefly looked at the young boy sitting on the couch, unwrinkled his forehead, and leaned forward almost all of the way out of the chair, almost standing. "Thank you, Mrs. Summers. That's kindly of you," he said, turning away from the boy to take his drink.

"I hope these two haven't been fillin' you with stories, Sheriff!" Micah laughed, looking at Iliana and Aaron sitting uncomfortably on the couch. She wondered what information the sheriff had gotten from Iliana.

"No, ma'am. We were just talkin'." The sheriff paused and took a drink from his glass and looked for a place to set it down. "Seems that Anna here doesn't remember – or doesn't want to remember," the sheriff wrinkled his forehead toward Iliana again before continuing, "her last name, or where her folks live. I haven't gotten no wheres with her yet. Anna, you sure you don't want to tell me where your folks are?"

Iliana looked pleadingly at Micah, hoping for intervention, but Micah's eyes, though more sympathetic, were just as inquiring as the sheriff's. Iliana turned to the sheriff, and weighing her words carefully, began. "Sheriff, Mara's Mom, I'm telling you the truth — it's all I know. I don't have a last name, and I don't know how I got to be here like this at your home. If I could tell you more, I would, because I know that you want to help me. I am sorry; I don't know what to tell you."

Micah tilted her head slightly, wondering. The voice sounded almost the same as Mara's — sweet and innocent, but the words were put together in a way that she had never heard Mara speak — with a deeper understanding than what she thought Mara was capable of. She thought that whoever Iliana had been raised by must have cared very deeply for her, to have imparted such maturity in a child so young. She turned to the sheriff, who sat quietly studying Iliana's features.

"Sheriff, I think she's telling the truth. It's the same thing she told me last night." Micah was shaking her head slowly, wondering what the sheriff's reaction would be. She had already grown very fond of Iliana, and wanted to be involved in her care.

The sheriff leaned all the way back in the recliner, and began to rock slowly, thoughtfully. He had never seen such a beautiful child, and was impressed by her countenance. The sheriff had always considered himself a good judge of character, and had relied on his instinct in many similar situations. He weighed the information that he had gathered from his interrogation carefully, and decided that Iliana was probably telling the truth about what she knew. Whatever the answer to the mystery was, he suspected that it was not going to be easily revealed — not this morning anyway.

"Anna, honey, don't you fret about this." The sheriff leaned all the way forward, and pulled himself from the deep chair. "We'll find out where your folks are, and get you back home as soon as we can. Everything's gonna be all right now. In the meantime…" the sheriff stood up all the way, and looked around again for a place to set his glass.

"Sheriff, if it's okay, Iliana can stay here while you're searching," Micah blurted out as the sheriff paused, surprised at her own words.

Her mouth hung open as she watched the sheriff turn fully toward her, anticipating his reaction.

"Well, Mrs. Summers, that'd be mighty unusual. We usually let Child Protective Service handle a case like this, with her being a lost child an' all." The sheriff studied Micah's reaction, and turned to Iliana and Aaron still sitting on the couch. "Would it be all right for these two to run outside an' play for awhile, Mrs. Summers? I'd like to have a word with you." The sheriff turned again to Mrs. Summers, nodding his head slowly up and down.

"Iliana, would you mind taking Aaron out to play for a while? Why don't you give him a push on the tire swing? He loves to swing!" Micah smiled as the two children jumped from the couch, heading to the back door.

"Come – on, – 'Liana, – let's – go – swing!" Aaron glanced back at Iliana to make sure she was following, and then ran out the door. Micah listened until she heard the spring on the screen door slam the door shut, and then turned to face the sheriff. He had placed the glass on the end table, and was standing in front of the couch. His white undershirt peeked out around the neck of his starched uniform, covering a broad chest resting on top of an ample belly which had grown each year since his college football days had ended. He seemed uncomfortable standing in the room alone with Micah. She smiled up at the sheriff, hoping to ease his discomfort.

"Mrs. Summers, do you know anything more 'bout how Anna got here than what you told me on the phone?" The sheriff was turning his hat around the brim with his fingers, slowly, as if wiping something from the edge of the brim. Micah's smile had distracted him. She was a striking woman, about five foot seven and just a little on the thin side, not showing the usual signs of a woman who had three young children. Her long brown hair was piled up in a bun loosely pulled high on her head with whispers of it loose and falling around her face. Her pale blue eyes had a trace of wrinkles beginning to show above her high cheek bones. Her smile was wide and generous, and her full lips flattened as the smile's pressure pulled them against the surface of her straight, white teeth. She wore a blue patterned apron over a long white dress that was frayed at the bottom, showing her worn tennis shoes tied neatly in perfect bows. The sheriff caught himself staring at her eyes, nervously glanced down at the floor, and then back at Micah.

"Sheriff," Micah began, slowly shaking her head from side to side while moving her glance out the window towards the hackberry tree, "I just don't know. The kids all told me the same thing, that she just showed up while they were playing. None of them saw where she came from or anything – just all at once she was there." She turned back to the sheriff, who was watching her intently. "I just didn't know what to do. I asked her about herself, but she really doesn't seem to remember who she is or where she came from. She seems like a really bright little girl, I don't know if she's hiding from someone, or afraid to tell me the truth, or if she even knows it." Micah looked carefully at the sheriff, trying to gauge his reaction, and continued, "I swear, Sheriff, I just don't have any idea. She seems to be plenty happy here, for now. I saw her cry a little bit when the kids got on the bus, but other than that, she seems to be okay. She gets along really well with Mara, my little six year old girl. They look to be about the same age. As a matter of fact, she seemed pretty upset when I told her she couldn't go to school with her this morning – I thought she was gonna panic! That's why I thought," Micah paused, again trying to guess what the sheriff was thinking, "maybe she could stay here till you find her family. I mean, she does seem comfortable and all, and I could keep her safe and keep trying to find out more information as she gets more used to me." Micah pulled an old wooden chair from the corner and sat down carefully, smiling again at the sheriff, hoping to draw him into a conversation before he rendered a quick "No."

The sheriff took the cue. He looked behind him and sat down carefully on the couch. Letting a runaway child stay with someone who was practically a stranger went against all of his training, but Micah's smile had disarmed him, and he didn't want to say no to such an attractive woman. "Well now, Mrs. Summers, I don't know if I can let her stay or not. I mean, she really ought to be placed with professional people that know how to deal with this and all." The sheriff paused, placing his hat on the couch beside him. "I don't really know much about you, or your family..." the sheriff lied, having found out as much as he could about the woman and her children who had moved out to the abandoned house by the hunting camp two months ago. He had asked around, trying to understand what circumstances had brought the Summers out to Hondo County. He had heard all about how Benjamin Summers, fancy city attorney, had left Micah without a dime, and only her house to live in. He had heard the gossip that Summers had taken his money and sailed off on his new boat, with his twenty year something paralegal, not even leaving a phone number to contact him, just a post office box in the city. "Midlife crisis," the locals said, as they wagged their heads in disgust, "leaving that woman and her three kids like that — he ought to be strung up!"

He knew that Micah had to sell the house in town so that she could have enough money to live on, and that she was struggling to make it with her three children. "...so why don't you tell me a little about yourself."

Micah looked at the sheriff, remembering how he had driven out to meet her when she first moved in. "Howdy, ma'am, just checkin' to see if everything's alright out here." She had appreciated his presence, and had been glad that he had come by. Lord knew, she had felt pretty insecure about moving out to where she didn't know a single soul. The house had been vacant for years, left behind when her great uncle Marshall had passed away and her great aunt had gone to the nursing home. She had never seen it before, but knew of its existence from the stories her cousins had told about spending summers out in the country with their grandparents. She remembered how thankful she was when her cousin Amanda, the executor of the estate, offered the house to her after she heard about Benjamin's leaving.

"Well, Sheriff," Micah began, clearing her throat with a slight cough, "Me and the kids moved out here to start a new life. My husband left me recently, and after talking it over with my children, I decided that maybe the country would be a good place to live for a while." Micah looked down, gathering her thoughts, wondering how much information she should give the sheriff. Looking back up, she offered a quick smile before beginning again. "Like I told you when you first came out, the house had belonged to family, and it seemed like a good move. I have two other children besides Aaron, who you already saw today. Mara — she's six and Ben, he's almost ten and in fourth grade. They're both off at school down at Hondo Elementary — they ride the bus." Micah paused again, waiting to see if the sheriff had any questions yet. He shifted slightly, nodded his head, and said nothing, so Micah continued. "I plan on finishing my degree plan at the community college in the spring, after we get settled down here. I only lack a few credits from getting my secondary education certificate." Micah's mind flashed back to the foolishness that she had been warned about by her father of leaving the University before she finished. Benjamin had been so handsome, so kind, and so impulsive when he proposed. "For now, I just plan on staying out here and taking care of the kids. The last few months have been hard on them." Micah paused deliberately, waiting for the sheriff to ask before volunteering any other information.

The sheriff studied Micah carefully. He already knew everything she had told him. He had let his mind drift off, watching the way that Micah's mouth moved as she talked, and was taken back a little when she paused. He had to mentally rewind her words before formulating a question. The sheriff had already decided that Iliana could stay out here with the Summers, but he didn't want to give the appearance of too hasty of a decision. "So, Mrs. Summers, you don't think that an extra child around would be more of a burden to you?" The sheriff smiled reassuringly, unwittingly indicating his decision prematurely.

"No, Sheriff, not at all. In fact, she'd be a good friend to my little girl — I mean 'till we find her family and all. No burden at all!" Micah realized that she had won the sheriff's decision, and smiled brightly. "We'd love to have her stay!"

The sheriff slowly stood up, and placed his hat on top of head, pulling the brim slightly to the front. "Well, this goes against what I ought to do, but I guess it won't hurt for the little girl to stay with you while I do some preliminary investigatin'." The sheriff took a small pad from his front pocket, and began to write in it. "I'm gonna check first with the neighbors, and see if any of them might know something, and maybe over at the huntin' camp, and I'll ask around town a little. No use making a big deal of this yet, and gettin' Child Protective involved. They'd just come get her and put her in some foster home right away, instead of waitin' a little. I'm sure that her family'll show up pretty quick, and we'll get 'em right back together." The sheriff finished writing and put the notepad back into his pocket. "In the meantime, I'm sure she'll be safe out here with you all." The sheriff smiled and started heading to the door.

Micah joined him, and reached out to open the wooden door. "Thank you, Sheriff, for coming out and all. It's real reassuring to know that you're here when we need you. We'll take good care of Iliana, and I'll call if she remembers any more information."

"Okay, Mrs. Summers. 'Bye, now." The sheriff tipped his hat and walked briskly towards his unit, whistling an unfamiliar tune as he left. He opened the door and slid in behind the steering wheel, pausing to give a quick wave before slamming the door and starting the engine. Micah gave a satisfied smile as she watched the car head down toward the mailbox and turn right, heading to the east, throwing a cloud of dust behind it as it went.

Hondo

"My, Aaron, you look very nice!" Micah admired her son as she dipped the comb under the bathroom faucet. Aaron stood straight and proud, with his chin down and his chest stuck out, his eyes peering upward as he tried to see what Micah was doing to his hair. "You're almost as big as Ben!"

"Big – like – Ben?" Aaron asked, straining to see the comb pass through his hair. He admired his brother more than anyone, especially since his dad was not around anymore.

"Yes, Aaron, as big as your brother." Micah stepped back to admire her work, and smiled satisfactorily. Aaron was growing up fast. The farm air seemed to have given him a fresh growth spurt. Brushing her hair back from her forehead and smoothing her cress, Micah called, "Come on, let's go to town." She opened the door to let Aaron and Iliana out, and followed them onto the porch. Trips to town were rare and were a treat, especially this day. For the first time since moving to Hondo,

Aaron held his mom's attention with little competition. Iliana, though along for the ride, posed no permanent threat to Aaron, and he was enjoying her company.

"Come — on, — 'Liana!" Aaron raced ahead to the brown Oldsmobile that Micah had bought at the Hondo car lot. She missed the old BMW, but she was happy to trade for the much newer car that, although not nearly as attractive, she knew would need much less maintenance. Aaron pulled desperately at the handle, unable to extend it far enough to open the door. Catching up, Iliana reached out and lifted the latch, allowing Aaron to finish pulling the door open. The two climbed into the back seat, and searched for the ends of the seat belts.

"Make sure you two get buckled in!" Micah cheerfully warned, as she slid into the front behind the steering column. Turning the key, she put her hand up to the air vent, waiting for the air to cool down before shutting the door.

"Mara's Mom," called out Iliana, "will we be going close to Mara's school?"

Iliana looked apprehensive, hoping to be near wherever Mara was. She studied Micah's eyes through the rearview mirror.

"Yes, honey. We'll be going right past it!" Micah spoke to the image in the mirror while heading down the dirt driveway toward the mailbox. She wondered about Iliana's worried look.

"Can we stop to see her?" Iliana's eyes stayed focused on the mirror. She had been excited about leaving the farmhouse since morning, and now Micah was beginning to suspect why. "I really miss her!"

Micah turned right, to the east, and continued down the road, watching the dust fly up behind her. She wondered if it would ever rain. "No, Iliana, I'm sorry. But we'll get back in time to meet her at the bus stop." Micah glanced back at Iliana and decided to offer a reward. "Tell

"This hose comes with the washers already in it, Mrs. Summers. I don't think you'll need one of those," Henry said as he carefully studied the ends of the hose. He turned to the register, and after pushing a few keys, turned back to Micah, smiling again. "That'll be six dollars and thirty five cents, tax an' all."

Micah reached into her purse, pulled out a five and two ones, and handed the money to Henry. Looking to the back of the store, she called out, "Aaron, Iliana, come on kids. It's time to go." While Henry counted out the change, Micah watched as the two children came bounding back up the aisle from where she had last seen them. "Did Aaron get into any mischief?" she asked Iliana, with a mock stern look on her face.

"No ma'am!" Iliana's smile lit up her face as she presented Aaron to his mom.

"No – ma'am! No – mischief!" Aaron rocked back and forth with his hands in his pockets, looking outside the door. "Go – get – ice – cream?" he asked, looking up with a smile spreading across his entire face.

"Those are two fine looking kids, Mrs. Summers. The oldest already back in school?" Henry asked, as he handed her the sixty five cents. Henry remembered always seeing Micah with all three of her children in tow, and missed seeing Ben.

"Oh, no, Hank! I mean, yes, Ben's in school, but this little girl's not Mara, not mine – she's in school, too. This is Iliana," Micah paused, wondering how to explain the beautiful girl in front of her. "She's, uh, staying with us for a while." Iliana looked up at the proprietor and smiled shyly.

"Why, hello there, Iliana. You sure are pretty – kinda like Mrs. Summers, here." Henry glanced over at Micah and quickly looked back at Iliana, blushing slightly, surprised at his own boldness. "Hey! Tell you what. How would you two like a piece of candy?" Henry smiled brightly at the two children and reached under the counter for an old ice cream bucket filled with hard wrapped candies.

"Hank, no!" Micah began, thinking about the Dairy Queen she had already promised the children.

"Candy!" Aaron's smile spread across his face, and his two hands shot out of the pockets in his overalls, forming a bowl with the two of them pressed together while jumping from one foot to the other. "Candy! – Candy!"

Micah took a deep breath, and finished as she exhaled "Well, all right. But just one, Aaron. That's all you get." Both Aaron and Henry politely ignored the directions, and Aaron's hands filled with red, yellow and blue hard candies. Henry patted him on the head and turned to Iliana, who was standing back, watching Micah for a signal.

"Go ahead, Iliana, you too!" Micah smiled as the young girl reached carefully into the bucket and pulled out a solitary pink candy.

"Thank you!" Iliana said, and gave Henry an appreciative smile.

"Thank – u" Aaron mumbled, his mouth already sucking on a blue disk, as he stuffed the rest of the candies carefully into his pockets.

Henry turned to Micah and held out the bucket. "Mrs. Summers?" he asked.

"No, but thank you anyway. You've been a big help, Hank. I really appreciate it, but I need to finish up here in town and get on back to the house before the school bus gets there..." and looking at her purchase, continued, "...and before we run out of clean clothes!"

Henry put the bucket away and smiled broadly again. "Okay, Mrs. Summers! Thanks for coming in to Slaughter's. Glad to help anytime!"

Micah pushed open the heavy wooden door, jingling the bell again with the movement. She held it open until Iliana and Aaron had cleared the door, and then led the two of them back to the car and buckled them in.

The Dairy Queen was only three blocks away, down at the only other light in town at the intersection of the highway running north from Rockdale up toward Waco. Micah pulled into the lot, and parked as far under an old huisache tree as she could to shade the car, and walked towards the store with Aaron and Iliana. The air conditioning was a welcoming blast of cold air greeting them as they went in. The place had always been crowded and bustling with children on Micah's other visits, but today, with all of the other kids in school, it was strangely quiet. Iliana followed Aaron as he climbed up onto a stool at the counter and carefully took her place beside him.

The girl at the counter looked as though she could barely be out of high school. "Hi, kids! What can I get for you?" She smiled at the two eager faces as she stopped wiping the countertop and leaned over to get at eye level with the young patrons. Her dark brown hair was layered in long, hanging curls and hung just inches from the counter as she looked from Aaron's excited little face to Iliana's contented smile.

"Two small dipped cones!" Micah spoke out, hoping to circumvent any lengthy discussions about what to order. "And a Diet Coke for me." Micah glanced at the clock on the wall and realized that they would have to hurry if they were going to meet Mara and Ben when the bus returned home. School would be letting out any minute, and even though their house was almost the last stop, she didn't think it would take more than forty minutes on the bus. She would have just enough time if there were no delays.

"Yeah! Ice – cream! Ice – cream!" Aaron cried excitedly, as Iliana sat beside him smiling quietly.

"Okay, honey, coming right up!" the young waitress said, softly tweaking Aaron's nose and returning Iliana's smile before turning away to prepare the order.

◆

Mara had been uncomfortable and nervous at school all day, causing her teacher to feel her forehead and consider calling her mother. The child didn't have a fever or any other symptoms, but she seemed to be more apprehensive than the other children. During lunch, she had picked at her food and seemed distracted. Miss Parker had taught first grade for several years and knew that something wasn't quite right. She wished that Mara's mother was coming to pick her up so that she could share her concerns. The quiet little girl did not appear at all to be the same bright, happy child she had met at the school's open house just the week before. "Good bye, Mara. I'll see you tomorrow!" Miss Parker called out as she helped Mara onto the bus and watched her walk to the back. Miss Parker smiled at the bus driver but didn't recognize her. She knew that the growth of the school had required the hiring of new staff, but was surprised at the youthful looking woman driver. "Keep an eye on her, if you would. She seems to be a little nervous." Miss Parker saw the driver look up at her from her clipboard and smile, and wondered if she had heard her or not.

Mara was relieved to see Ben board the bus shortly after her, but was disappointed when he took a seat up near the front. She wanted to call out to him to come and sit by her, but the noise of the children prevented her from even giving it an effort. She turned and stared out the window, feeling afraid and alone.

Thrown back in the seat as the bus lurched forward, Mara looked up to the front and saw the driver's young eyes watching, checking to see if her unfamiliarity with the clutch had dislodged any children. Mara felt the bus begin to roll down the slope leading from the parking lot to the street, and she turned to look out the window. She spotted the front of the uranium tanker growing quickly in front of her, and watched as the truck's cab silently began to jackknife from the tank, sliding sideways ever more slowly toward the bus. Mara's backpack fell to the floor as the bus accelerated, and she heard her own scream mix with dozens of others to drown out the squealing brakes and horn.

◆

"No!" The ice cream cone fell to the floor as Iliana jumped from her stool, staring out the window. The scream startled Aaron, whose ice cream fell off his cone as he tilted it in the confusion. "No!" Iliana shrieked again, still staring out the window.

Micah quickly set down her drink and rushed to Iliana. "What, honey! What is it?" The scream was frightening, as though coming deep from within her. Since meeting Iliana, Micah had never heard the child raise her voice except in laughter, and she was confused by the outburst. Looking around, she saw nothing alarming, but spied the ice cream splattered on the floor beneath the stool. "It's okay, honey. We'll get you a new cone. It's all right!" Micah glanced to the young waitress, who, taking her cue, quickly began to make another cone.

"My – ice – cream – fall – down!" Aaron cried emphatically. "It – all – dirty!"

"It's okay, Aaron. We'll get you a new one, too." Micah said comfortingly, as the waitress nodded her head in agreement.

Iliana collapsed on to her stool, and lowering her head in her arms, began sobbing. Micah put her arm around the child's shoulders softly. "It's okay, honey. Accidents happen. It's gonna be okay." She reached up and took the hurriedly made ice cream cone from the waitress and held it in front of the sobbing Iliana. "Here you go; here's a new cone. Go ahead, honey; it's okay." Micah continued, offering the cone to the quietly sobbing Iliana, who was not lifting her head from her arms.

"Thank – you," Aaron said over his pouting lip, and looked up, sad but appreciatively, at the cone being presented to him. He took it, and began to lick it while the waitress started to wipe the ice cream from the counter.

Iliana continued to sob almost silently as Micah rubbed her shoulders, not willing to take the replacement cone which was repeatedly offered. Micah looked up at the clock and realized that they would have to leave soon or risk being late for the bus's arrival. "Honey, could you wrap up about a dozen of those cookies over there for me to take?" The waitress stopped staring at Iliana's slumping form, and quickly smiled at Micah. She pulled a bag from under the counter, and counted out twelve of the cookies.

"How much is it?" she asked, standing up and reaching for her purse.

"That'll be six dollars, even,." The waitress said quietly. "Is she okay?"

Micah looked at Iliana, and wondered too. She thought about how Mara would be holding up under similar circumstances and decided to renew her efforts at reuniting Iliana with her family. No wonder Iliana was upset. How could she act any differently? "I think she's fine. She probably just misses her family," Micah offered without further explanation as she handed over the bills.

Micah reached to Aaron, pulled a napkin from the holder on the counter, and tried to wipe off the dripping ice cream from his chin and neck. "I – like – ice – cream!" Aaron said, happy, but still somewhat subdued. Micah helped him down from the stool, and turned to rubbing Iliana's back again.

"Come on, Iliana. We have to go now, or we'll be late for the bus." Micah watched as the young girl slowly lifted her head. "Come on, honey. We'll be there when Mara gets off the bus." Iliana slowly lifted her head and climbed off of the stool. She followed Aaron to the car without speaking, looking down the street anxiously as she walked.

Micah pulled out and drove the five blocks back to the light and took a left back toward the house. Pulling out on the street, she could see flashing lights up ahead near the school. She slowed as an officer waved her around a jackknifed tanker truck that was lying with the cab upright on the grass between the street and the Hondo Elementary parking lot. The bright aluminum tank had rolled over sideways in the street, slowly spilling pale yellow liquid onto the pavement. A sense of unexplained dread sucked her breath out as she came around the tanker. Anxiously, she passed the tanker, and finally could clearly see the scene ahead. Several men with yellow coats were hurrying toward the truck, dragging large heavy hoses. Two officers stood at the front of the tanker, talking to a man in uniform, while the sheriff stood in the middle of the street, directing oncoming traffic. "Thank God." Micah whispered, finally able to inhale. Micah could see no other vehicles involved in the accident, and there appeared to be no injuries. She let her breath out slowly, and reached to her shoulder strap, subconsciously checking to make sure it was attached. "Aaron? Iliana?" she called, looking back in the rear view mirror, "See why you always wear your seatbelts?"

"Wow," Aaron said, pushing his hands against the window while looking back at the overturned rig.

Iliana's hands and face were up against her window too, looking intently at the scene surrounding the tanker. Micah thought she could see small tears again forming in her eyes and silently renewed her vow to try to find the child's family. She thought she saw from the corner of her eye the sheriff smile and wave as she passed by, but didn't turn to respond, keeping both of her hands firmly gripped to the steering wheel and her eyes straight ahead as she slowly accelerated down the road. Only once did she lift her eyes to the mirror to view the shrinking accident behind her, and again she felt relief that she could see no sign of injuries. Turning her eyes back to the road leading home, she carefully accelerated to meet the school bus at the stop.

Home

Squinting at the sound and dust, Aaron and Iliana stepped back briefly as the door opened, and then moved forward to the bottom of the steps. They didn't notice the young driver smile and wave at them as they looked up excitedly, waiting for the first sign of the passengers to step off of the bus.

"Hey, short stuff, what's up?" Ben put his hand up high on the silver colored pole next to the bus door, and feet in the air, swung his body down the steps. He landed squarely on the first step, facing Aaron. Ben's hair was mussed, and his shirttail was hanging out as he stepped off of the bus. He bent down and picked up Aaron high into the air, spinning him around before setting him on the ground. "Want a piggyback ride?" Ben offered. Bending down, he looked up at Iliana and greeted, "Hey!" Iliana smiled at Ben briefly, watching as Aaron laughed and climbed up on his brother's back, and then she returned to staring at the steps for a familiar face.

"You sure you're okay?" The bus driver had turned to face the back of the bus and Iliana could see her addressing an approaching child. "You want me to walk you to the house?"

"I'm all right, just a little bump." Mara appeared, holding a dripping paper towel to her forehead, smiling gratefully at the driver. "Thank you for taking me home."

"Okay, Mara, I hope to be here in the morning!" The driver returned Mara's smile and patted her back as she made her way carefully down the steps.

Mara looked up from the bottom step. "Iliana!" Mara smiled brightly and stepped down to meet her, not even noticing the door closing loudly behind and the bus pulling away. "I thought you'd be gone!" Mara pulled her hand from her forehead, and wrapped her arms around her friend, wetting the back of Iliana's shirt with the cold paper towel. The two hugged briefly, and then stepped back to see one another.

"Oh, no, Mara, what happened to your head?" Iliana's face reflected deep concern as she reached her hand out to gently touch Mara's forehead.

"I'm okay, I just bumped my head on the seat. A big truck almost hit the bus!" Mara's eyes opened wide as she remembered the truck sliding toward her, barely missing the back of the bus where she sat. Mara remembered the bus driver asking "Is everyone okay?" after slamming on the brakes. She had just been able to accelerate past the truck, not having seen it coming down the street until she was half way into the intersection. Mara, sitting in the last seat, had been thrown forward into the seat ahead of her, and had gotten a small bump on her head, the only injury on the bus. She had been grateful when the driver pulled ice from a cooler at the front of the bus, and wrapped it inside a brown paper towel, and placed it on her forehead. The damp, cool towel had comforted her on the long ride home.

The two girls turned to wave at the school bus as it pulled into the road to the hunting camp. The bus backed up, and turning around, headed back towards Hondo. "Come on, Iliana, let's get home!" Mara raced Iliana towards the house, holding the paper towel to her head as she ran, long pigtails flapping at her back.

Ben and Aaron were already sitting at the table, munching on cookies dripping with glasses of cold milk in front of them. Ben was excitedly telling about the near accident, his hands in the air imitating the two vehicles as they almost collided. Micah saw Mara holding the paper towel to her head and bent down to meet her.

"Hi, Mom! I'm home!" Mara threw herself into Micah's open arms and gave her a big hug with her free arm. Micah squeezed her hard before gently pushing her back and looking at her forehead.

"My goodness, Mara, are you okay?" Micah carefully pulled Mara's hand away from her head and studied the injury. "Ben told me you got hurt."

"I'm okay, it's just a little bump. The driver gave me a cold towel to put on it so it wouldn't swell up. Did Ben tell you about the crash?" Mara turned to her brother, who was pulling the glass of milk away from his mouth, leaving a white ring around his lips.

"Yeah, man, it was cool! That big truck came slidin' right at us and fell over right in front of the school. Boy, it was neat!" Ben grinned under his tussled hair and again began to demonstrate the action with his hands.

Micah smiled slightly at her son, and turned back to Mara, putting her fingers gently to the red, raised bump above her left eye. "Come on, honey, we got you some of those cookies you like from down at the Dairy Queen. Come on, Iliana, let's show Mara what we bought."

Mara and Iliana joined the two boys at the table and reached out for cookies from the tray on the table. The ice cream middles of the cookie sandwiches were soft and runny, making the chocolate cookies limp, but the girls eagerly bit into them. The cool ice cream felt refreshing after the long afternoon, and they didn't mind the drips running down their chins. Iliana had not taken her eyes off Mara since she had gotten off of the bus. After Iliana saw Mara's bump was not serious, she had not spoken a word, satisfied to gaze at Mara with a contented smile.

Mara smiled back as she bit deep into her cookie, her eyes growing as big as her mouth. It felt good to be home; safe, secure, and sheltered. She had not felt this way since getting on the bus this morning.

"Mara, I missed you." Iliana put her cookie down and looked thoughtfully at Mara, staring deep into her eyes. "Please don't leave again! I was so worried about you."

"I missed you, too!" Mara smiled brightly at Iliana between bites of her cookie, glad to be home with her new friend. "Mom," she called out, "can I go up to my room and play with Iliana?"

"Sure, Mara, as soon as you finish your snack." Micah looked at the two, and felt glad that they were together. She hoped that it would turn out that Iliana was from close by so that they could visit often.

"Me – go – play – with – 'Liana – too." Called out Aaron, finishing the last drop of milk from his glass.

"No, not now. Let the girls play together for a while, okay, Aaron?" Micah watched as Aaron dropped his shoulders and stuck his chin deep in his chest, showing his disappointment. "Ben, why don't you take Aaron outside and play for a while. He's missed you a lot."

"Play – with – me?" Aaron wrinkled his nose and looked up hopefully at Ben.

"Sure, little guy, let's go!" Ben jumped from his chair and headed to the back door, with Aaron right behind him.

"You boys be careful — and stay away from the hunting camp!" Micah hollered as the boys scampered out the door.

"Sure thing, Mom!" Micah heard Ben's yell fade, as they disappeared in a burst of energy off the back porch.

"Okay, Mom. All done! Can we go up now?" Mara was cleaning the last of the ice cream from her face.

"Sure thing." Micah smiled as the two girls rose from their chairs and took each other's hands to head up the stairs. "You girls play nice, okay?" she added needlessly, knowing that it was the boys who were much more apt to get into mischief.

Micah rose from the table, stretching her long arms over her head. She listened upstairs for Mara and Iliana, and hearing them playing quietly, went to the living room. Micah picked up the phone and dialed hesitantly, not wanting to make the call, but knowing that she had to. "Hello, is the sheriff in?" Taking the phone, she paced nervously around the room, looking out the window to check on Aaron and Ben. "Yes, Sheriff, this is Micah Summers. I was checking to see if you had found out anything about Iliana yet." She spied the boys playing near the chicken pen, throwing rocks down into the ravine that led to the hunting camp, watching as Aaron tried hard to copy his big brother's motions. "No, she's doing fine. She's been crying a little. I think she's missing her family." Aaron bent down to pick up a rock, and threw it as hard as he could. "No, nothing. She still acts as though she knows nothing about her family or where she's from." Micah saw Ben point out something on the ground from where Aaron had just picked up his rock, and Aaron bent over carefully. "No, Sheriff, nothing at all." She turned her attention away from the boys and glanced back up the stairs, watching towards the top of the stairs at Mara's door as she thought of Iliana. "No, it won't be a problem at all. I'm glad to be of help."

Micah hung up the phone and slowly sat on the couch, sighing deeply, and looked out the window to where the boys had been playing.

The house was just the right kind of quiet, with the slight murmur of the girls upstairs and the boys outside, and it gave Micah the chance to stop and think. Life had been difficult since Benjamin had left. The boys had taken it very hard, even though he had not been around much the last two to three years, not since Aaron was born.

Even so, the children had all worshipped their dad and the precious little time he gave them. He had built a successful law practice; too successful, and the family had taken a back seat. On the rare occasions in the spring when Micah had been able to have a conversation with him, it had not gone well. Mostly arguments about him never being home, never spending time with the kids. Micah had thought that Mara would take his leaving the hardest. She had been closest to him, and had often stayed awake late at nights just to run down and give him a kiss when he finally came in from work, waiting for her dad to tuck her in before falling off to sleep. But Mara took the realization that he was gone with resolve, drawing on an inner strength that Micah envied.

Micah seldom let herself think about Benjamin, having tried hard to leave that part of her behind — even selling the house to help erase the memories. Micah felt a small tear slowly make a trek across her cheekbone, picking up speed as it rolled down her face. She set her jaw firmly to meet the tear, and brushed it away quickly as it came to rest on her tensed muscle. She turned her gaze quickly toward the stairs, fighting back any new tears that might try to escape. She was determined to make a good life for her children, and she was not going to let the memory of their dad take away from their happiness. Since moving to the farm, the boys had become happy again, laughing easily as they played together. Ben was Aaron's new idol, replacing his dad. The two boys were inseparable. Mara… Well, Mara had slowly adjusted to life without her dad. She was the one who had comforted Micah in those hard weeks, placing her arms around her neck and sitting on her lap, telling endless made up stories, all with happy fairy tale endings. In her dark moments, Micah had come to rely on Mara's strength, and even now she longed for her daughter's comfort.

Micah stood slowly, and carefully wiped the wrinkles out of her dress that had formed while she was sitting. She bit her bottom lip softly, and turned to go upstairs to try to talk to Iliana again about her family, determined not to let the feelings deep within her have another opportunity to escape.

"Mom!" Aaron's voice hollered as the screen door opened, and then quickly slammed shut. "I — caught — a — lizard!" Aaron appeared in the living room smiling broadly. He held his right hand up high, gently squeezing his thumb and finger together. Between them wiggled something small and green, with a tail thrashing back and forth. Aaron was moving fast toward his mom with the captured prey. Ben followed his younger brother, his face showing pride at the accomplishment.

"Oh, my gosh, Ben, what is that thing?" Micah back peddled furiously, trying to stay out of arms reach of the excited Aaron, taking her eyes off the wiggling creature only long enough to see Ben smiling widely behind his brother with a too amused face.

"It — a — lizard!" shouted Aaron again excitedly. "See?" Aaron had cornered Micah up against the wall next to the stairs and was still approaching.

"That's nice, Aaron, it's...beautiful! Now put it away, Aaron, please, quickly!" Micah was wiggling more than the reptile as she tried to stay clear of it. She thought she saw a large, red balloon emerge from just under its throat, and gasped. "Oh, God, Ben, help Aaron take that thing away, please!" Aaron and Ben were beginning to convulse in laughter at what they thought was their mother's mock terror. "Please, Ben, please!" Micah screamed, not taking her eyes off the lizard, now no more than a foot from her face.

Ben began to suspect that his mother was being serious, and grabbed Aaron from behind with both arms, slowly pulling him back while still laughing. "Mom, can I have one of those old jars under the sink to put him in? I told Aaron he could keep him."

"It — a — lizard, — Mom. See?" Aaron was still trying to move forward towards his mom while slowly being pulled backward by Ben, determined to share his good news with Micah.

"Yes, Aaron, that's very nice. Go with Ben, hurry! Before it gets away. Yes, Ben, anything you can find. That's very nice of you!" Micah said without taking a breath, trying to smile as the lizard retreated from her face. She closed her eyes briefly as she saw the boys turn to head toward the kitchen, and decided that it was a good time to go and talk to Iliana. "Ben, you make sure that thing doesn't escape in the house, you hear me?!" she shouted back as she quickly made her way up the stairs.

Mara and Iliana were sitting on the floor, joined in a circle with Mara's two Barbies. In the middle was the gray ceramic tea set that Mara had gotten for her third Christmas. As Micah opened the door, Mara was holding up a cup to Workout Barbie, offering her the tea. "It's wonderful, Barbie, and only two calories — so you don't get too fat."

Micah walked in and was able to smile again, quickly forgetting the three inch reptile that had traumatized her only moments before. Her smile was returned by the two girls sitting on the braided rug. "Hey, girls, you having a tea party?"

"Yes, Mom, you want to play too?" Mara looked up and smiled, and scooted her bottom over to make room.

"Sure." Micah squeezed between Tropical Barbie and Mara, and smiled at Iliana sitting across from her. She watched as Mara carefully placed a saucer in front of Micah's folded legs and held up the cup to Iliana to fill with make believe tea.

"How many spoons of sugar do you want?" Mara offered, as Iliana slowly filled Micah's cup with pretend tea.

"None, thank you," Micah answered, looking cautiously at Workout Barbie, "I'd better watch my figure!"

The three laughed and giggled as they drank their imaginary tea and ate pretend cookies, making sure that the dolls had a share in everything. Mara had forgotten all about the bump on her head, and seemed to be enjoying Iliana's company immensely. The two girls seemed so comfortable together, as though they had been friends forever.

"I talked to the sheriff again today," Micah started, glancing up to watch Iliana's eyes before continuing, "and he said that he hadn't been able to find your family yet." Micah looked carefully at Iliana, trying to read her reaction. Iliana returned her gaze with an unfathomable expression that showed neither surprise nor disappointment. "Iliana," Micah began slowly, "do you remember anything yet at all about your family, where they live, what your last name is?"

Iliana looked intently, and them shook her head slowly, "No, Mara's Mom, nothing at all." Sensing disappointment in Micah's eyes, she added cheerfully, "I'm sorry. I'll keep trying!"

Micah looked at Mara, who was watching Iliana breathlessly. She saw her smile and move closer to Iliana, and prayed that her daughter would not take the inevitable separation too hard. The two quickly began a conversation with the dolls about their hair, and Micah decided to let the sheriff worry about Iliana's family. In the meantime, she would do her best to just make Iliana comfortable and happy.

"Iliana, I guess you'll be staying here with Mara until the sheriff finds your family. It's a good thing you two are about the same size!" Micah stood up and pretended to wipe cookie crumbs from her dress. "Mara, why don't you let Iliana help you pick out clothes for school tomorrow, and lay them on the dresser," Micah began, and then considered what possibilities tomorrow held. "And see if you can find some clothes for Iliana to wear to school, too."

"You mean Iliana can go to school with me?" Mara jumped up excitedly, taking both of Iliana's hands and pulling her up.

"Well, I'm not sure, but it kinda looks that way right now, at least until the sheriff calls." Micah wondered how long it might take for Iliana's family to be found. "Why don't you try that blue plaid dress that ties in the back on Iliana, and see if your blue denim shoes will fit her, okay?"

Mara and Iliana headed quickly to the closet and Mara reached high on her tiptoes to reach the string dangling down from the light bulb high above the clothes. Micah turned to leave the two excited girls, happy that they seemed so contented, envious of their youthful exuberance. "Well, girls, I hate to leave such wonderful company, but I've got to start supper," she called out as she left the door and headed down the steps to the kitchen.

Mara had Iliana try on every dress and each pair of shoes in the closet. The two finally agreed that Micah's suggestion had been the best after all, and they carefully laid out the clothes for the next day. Mara seemed so thankful to have a friend out on the farm.

"Iliana, I'm so glad you're going to school with me. We'll have so much fun together!" Mara beamed at Iliana, not wanting to take her eyes off her beautiful new friend.

"I'm glad too! I don't ever want to be away from you." Iliana reached out and gave Mara a hug.

The two stood holding each other's hands, but gradually Mara's smile faded into a worried look. "Iliana, will you ever leave me?" Mara didn't understand her mom's concern about Iliana's family. She innocently knew only what she felt — that being together made both of them happy. She hoped that Iliana would never have to leave.

"No, Mara, I don't think so. I hope we will always be together!" Iliana smiled reassuringly.

Mara's concern deepened. Her forehead wrinkled as she looked intently at Iliana, seeking more assurance. "Do you miss your mom and dad?" Iliana's smile faded as she breathed in deeply, unsure of how to answer. "I miss my dad — I wish he was here," Mara continued, and Iliana saw a small tear begin to form under Mara's eye as her gaze dropped to the floor.

Iliana squeezed Mara's hand and began, "I'm sorry, Mara, I wish he was here too."

"Will your dad come back for you?" Mara eyes returned to Iliana, searching for an answer.

Iliana stared hard at Mara, wondering how to answer. Since being trapped in the box, Iliana had become increasingly confused. She had experienced feelings that she had never before felt, and for the first time ever was uncertain of how to continue. Before, everything had seemed very simple. She existed to help Mara in her life, to protect her, to guide her on her path, to help her to know the difference between right and wrong. She had suffered with her, and felt very deeply the separation that Mara had felt from her dad. But never before had she experienced the loneliness of separation from Mara.

Never before had she had to answer questions so directly, and felt unsure of how to answer any but the simplest of questions. Did she miss her dad? She didn't even know. She felt her father's presence, knew that he was there, watching her, guiding her, but still she felt more distant from him since she had been trapped. Yes, she missed him. Her physical presence had made her unsure of how to continue, and she desperately wanted him to guide her in the choices she had to make. Choices — something that she had only briefly known. Before, everything was clear, almost every decision already made, her only choice to carry out the task she was given. In that existence, the only pain was that shared from the choices made by others, never her own. Now, each choice carried the possibility of her inflicting pain on others, each decision presented an almost limitless possibility of choices. She longed desperately to return to her previous existence, before the trap, to its security, never having to make a choice, never having to risk hurting someone she loved.

"Mara, I have to tell you something." Iliana shuddered, slowly beginning to realize the possibility of the impact of the choice that she was starting to make.

"What, Iliana?" Mara asked quietly.

Iliana looked deep into Mara's eyes and saw an innocence as pure as her own, an innocence of not yet being responsible for the pain caused by poorly made decisions. Iliana realized at that moment that Mara, too, shared with Iliana not having made a decision to deliberately hurt, to deceive. She and Mara shared in that perfect innocence of youth, and Iliana hesitated, uncertain whether to continue or not.

"Mara, Aaron was right. He saw something that neither you nor Ben saw down under the hackberry tree. He saw my…wings."

"Your wings?" Mara stared at Iliana, her eyes wide, her small hand rising to her mouth.

"Yes, Mara, before you found me in the box, I had wings. You couldn't see me, but I was watching over you, trying to protect you. I saw a bullet coming toward you, and I rushed to push you out of the way. I don't know what happened, but suddenly the box came crashing down on top of me, and I was trapped, in the dark."

"What happened to your wings?" Mara asked.

"I don't know. When you opened the box, I was surprised, because you could see me, and when I tried to fly away, nothing happened. Mara, I don't think that I'm supposed to be here, and I feel a little lost – except when I am with you."

Mara stared at Iliana intently, trying to comprehend what was being said. The information had come unexpectedly, and she was unsure about what to make of this revelation. Mara slowly tilted her head, and asked in amazement, "Are you an angel, Iliana?"

"An angel, Mara. Your guardian angel."

"My guardian angel?"

"Yes, but now I don't know what to do. I couldn't protect you when you were hurt in the bus, and I am afraid. I am afraid that I might do the wrong thing, Mara, that if I do what is wrong, you will be hurt." Iliana stopped, wondering if even now she had done what was wrong. Should she have told Mara? What would happen now? She didn't have a clue. She desperately searched Mara's eyes for signs that she had hurt her, for signs of pain.

"Iliana? Don't be afraid. I'll help you. I'll watch over you." Mara carefully took Iliana's hand in her own and smiled. "I always knew you were there, but I never saw you before. You are so beautiful. Thank you, Iliana, for being my angel."

The Lizard

"Come on, guys, everyone to bed!" Micah yelled up the stairs from the kitchen. She could hear footsteps running up and down the hall over her head as she finished up the supper dishes.

"Okay, Mom. Almost done!" Ben called out. Micah had given Ben the responsibility for making sure Aaron had gotten cleaned up and ready for bed. Ben had grown in many ways over the summer, and seemed to be very mature for his nine years, helping out and hardly ever complaining. Micah knew this age would not last forever as the teenage years loomed near, but she was appreciative of it for now.

The two girls had sat quietly at supper, smiling at one another and giggling as if they had a secret to hide. They had helped clear the table while their brothers bathed, and should have been finished getting ready for bed by now.

"Mara? Iliana? You two all ready?" Micah called out again.

"Just about!" Micah could hear Mara's voice along with her footsteps hurrying down the hall toward her bedroom. Micah listened as all of the footsteps gradually came to a stop, and decided to give everyone a few moments to settle down before she went up to say prayers. It had been a long, tiring day, yet she felt happy. She was concerned about the eventual outcome of Iliana, but was thankful that she was here, for Mara.

It felt good to be back in the rhythm of school again, and she was looking forward to quiet fall days alone with Aaron while Ben and Mara were away at class. She was even beginning to feel good about Benjamin being gone, not having to worry what time, or even if, he was coming home, not having to deal with making up explanations to the kids about their father's absence. It was hard for her even to remember missing him, and the hurt and anger were more memory than real anymore.

Micah felt good about the decisions she had made since Benjamin had left, and she was beginning to feel more and more confident of life on her own with the children. She had planned carefully, and had just enough money left over from the sale of the home in town to start school in the spring. With the help of a few student loans Micah felt sure she could finish her degree without having to work. She worried about Aaron being in day care, but knew that there was nothing else she could do while she finished her degree. Besides, she told herself, Aaron was a survivor. He always landed right side up.

Micah finished sweeping the crumbs from under the table and decided to rest for a few minutes before heading upstairs to tuck in the children. She lay on the couch and put her feet up, relishing the quiet of the farm. In the distance, she could hear the mournful cry of a dove, perhaps calling to its lost mate. Closing her eyes briefly, Micah wondered how it, too, would recover.

"Mom," Micah opened her eyes to see Aaron standing in his nightshirt and socks, reaching out his hand to her shoulder. "Mom."

"Yes, Aaron, what is it? You're supposed to be in bed." Micah sat up on the couch and smiled at the small boy in front of her, and marveled at how quietly he could have come down the stairs.

"Mom, – look." Aaron held out a jar to her, half filled with grass and covered with a lid poked full of holes. She stiffened slightly, remembering her earlier encounter, and hoped to herself that whatever had been inside had not escaped.

"Lizard – sleep – with – eyes – open?" Aaron held out the jar pleadingly to Micah, being so careful not to shake or disturb it. His eyes were not on the jar or its contents, but on Micah, searching, waiting for an answer. Micah looked at the boy's eyes, and then turned to look at the jar and its contents. Inside, the grass had been placed carefully, arranged to form a nest. In the center was a small white plastic cap, filled with water, and what looked like breadcrumbs were scattered on the bottom amid the grass. There was a forked brown stick rising from the bottom to the lid that had two or three leaves still attached. Lying in the grass on its side, with its eyes open, was the green lizard.

"Let me see, Aaron." Micah carefully took the jar and brought it close to her, thankful for the sturdy glass. She looked closely, first at the lizard, and then at the contents of the jar, and saw the love and care with which the items had been arranged. She carefully shook the jar, waiting for the lizard to jump at her.

"I don't know, Aaron. I don't know if it's asleep or not." She again carefully shook the jar.

"Lizard – sleep – with – eyes – open?" Aaron asked again, his voice becoming stronger, demanding. Micah looked at the boy, now staring intently at the jar. She turned to follow his gaze back to the lizard. Her disgust had disappeared, and she hoped that the small creature would move. She thought to herself that she would even be happy if it would puff up his orange neck and leap at her, anything, just so that it would move. She carefully shook the jar again, hoping.

She turned again toward Aaron, and saw him no longer staring at the jar, but at her, waiting for her answer. She placed the jar between them, and slowly, carefully removed the lid, shaking the jar one more time. "Move, jump, do something," she thought to herself as she carefully turned the jar to its side, moving the animal slowly. The lizard did not move on its own, but stared out to the sides with its eyes frozen open. Micah stared at it for a while, not wanting to turn back to Aaron, not wanting to tell him the truth.

"My – lizard – asleep?" Aaron had still not taken his eyes off of Micah, his voice now plaintive, hopeful, quiet. Micah closed her eyes against her own tears as she carefully placed the lid back on the jar.

"Aaron, I'm sorry," Micah began, turning her eyes to Aaron's. "Your pet's not asleep." She watched Aaron turn back to the lizard and reach out for the jar. She carefully handed him back the container, and watched as he took it and recreated her shaking actions. She wondered if he understood.

"Not – sleeping?" Aaron looked confused, and did not seem to want to give up hope.

Micah thought it would be better to just give him the news and not prolong the uncertainty. "No, Aaron, not – sleeping. I'm so sorry, Aaron, but your lizard has died."

"Died?" Aaron was still shaking the jar, waiting for movement. Micah was not certain that he understood

"Yes, Aaron, he's not living anymore."

"Not – living?"

Micah carefully picked up Aaron and sat him on her lap, slowly stroking his hair. She held him tight as she put her face close to his, both looking into the jar at the lizard. "Aaron, I'm sorry. Your lizard is dead."

Aaron sat quietly, still shaking the jar with his face tight up against the glass. "Aaron, we'll have to bury him."

"Bury – him?" Aaron continued his gaze at the jar.

"Yes, Aaron, we'll find a nice box and put the lizard in it, and dig a hole outside and put it in the ground."

"Why?"

Micah struggled, not sure how to continue, uncertain as to how much Aaron understood. "Aaron, sometimes things die. They aren't alive anymore. They can't move, or breathe, or do anything. It's real sad, because we will miss them, but we can't make them come back alive."

"Lizard – broken?"

"Yes, Aaron, kind of like that. It's broken and doesn't work."

"Mom – fix – lizard?" Aaron still shook the animal softly.

"No, Aaron, Mom can't fix the lizard. Nobody can. When things die, there is nothing anyone can do."

Aaron looked up at Micah, soft tears beginning to form in his eyes. He carefully set the jar on the table by the couch and crawled up into Micah's lap, his cheeks pushed up by his hands.

"Aaron – break – lizard."

Micah again fought back her own tears and held hard onto Aaron, feeling the boy's sadness. "No, Aaron. You didn't break the lizard. Look how good you took care of him. You gave him fresh grass and food and water, and look, Aaron, you put holes in the lid so that he would have plenty of air. I can tell how much you loved him – you really took good care your pet."

"Who — broke — lizard?" Tears were beginning to run down the little boy's cheeks as he snuggled closer to his mom.

"Nobody broke him, Aaron. Sometimes things just die, no matter how much we love them. Sometimes they get old; sometimes they get sick; sometimes they have an accident, and there's nothing that we can do."

"Nobody — broke — lizard? He — just — die?"

"Yes, Aaron, that's right. And there's nothing that we can do. Except that, while he's here, we can love him. Like you did, taking such good care of him. And then, when he dies, we can remember him, and that way we don't really lose him, because in a way, he's here with you in your memory." Micah felt Aaron sigh deeply in her arms, and wondered if he understood.

"O — kay." Aaron turned suddenly in her arms, and wrapped himself around her. "I — love — you, — Mom."

"I love you too, Aaron. I will always love you," Micah promised as she gently kissed Aaron on top of his head. "Come on, let's get up to bed."

School

Slowly at first, and then faster and faster, the two figures spun around silently. Eyes closed, arms stretched out, fingers pointing to the end of time, Mara and Iliana danced in the morning grass. The rising sun warmed their skin, and a soft wind blew their hair first into their faces and then behind them as they spun around and around. Their tiptoes seemed to be almost rising above the ground, whirling in a timeless motion as they floated effortlessly above a mist of endless joy.

"Here – comes – yellow – school – bus!" Aaron had climbed high into the tree, clinging tightly with one arm to a branch while pointing with his free hand towards an approaching cloud of dust. The shout woke the two girls from their dance, and taking each other's hand, they quickly grabbed their lunch sacks and backpacks.

"Come on, Aaron, climb down. I gotta get on the bus." Ben reached up and swung Aaron down from his perch in the tree, lowering him carefully to the ground.

Micah watched as the bus pulled into view and stopped, its door opening amid the swirling dust. "Good morning!" The gray haired man smiled openly at the children, his eyes looking enlarged through his thick glasses. "Hop on board!"

Ben glanced back at Micah, giving her a quick smile before turning to the bus and climbing the steps. Mara ran to her mom and threw her arms around her. "I love you, Mom!" Quickly she ran back to Iliana, and grabbing her hand, pulled her into the bus.

"Bye — Ben! Bye — Mara! Bye — 'Liana!" Aaron stood at the foot of the steps, watching as the door closed and the bus pulled away, disappearing down the road back toward Hondo. He waved his small hand until the bus faded from view, and then turned to face Micah. "O — kay, — Mom! All — gone!" Aaron said, wiping his hands together. Micah took Aaron's hand, and the two headed back toward the house together, arms swinging slowly as they walked.

The bus ride into town was long but uneventful, filling with laughter and more children's voices at each stop. The sheriff had called the Hondo Elementary principal the afternoon before and explained what he knew of Iliana's situation. They had agreed that she could attend school as a 'special guest' for a few days, and together they hoped that, perhaps, someone from the school would recognize her. Mara only knew she was happy to be with Iliana, and she looked forward to their day together.

The bus pulled up to the school, passing an area marked off with fluorescent orange cones where men in hardhats walked around. It stopped in front of the gym, where the children unloaded and piled into the gathering noise and confusion. Ben stopped just inside the door and entered a growing circle of young boys who were talking about the near accident on the bus the previous day. Mara led Iliana to a sign that had

'Miss Parker' written in large letters, with a brightly colored apple at the end of the name. They waited for a few moments, talking to each other until they heard the buzzing of the morning bell. Looking up, Mara saw the friendly face of Miss Parker approaching.

"Good morning, boys and girls. Let's all line up!" Miss Parker took the hand of a sandy haired boy, and smiled at the other children as they took their places behind him. Looking around at the children's faces smiling back at her, she sighted Iliana and came toward her. "Hi, Mara. Is this your friend?"

"Yes, ma'am, Miss Parker. This is Iliana!" Mara giggled and nervously bit on her finger as she turned toward Iliana, uncomfortable with the attention of being singled out.

"My goodness, you sure are a sweet thing!" Miss Parker thought that she had never seen such a beautiful child, and wondered how she could possibly be missing from her family. "Iliana, Mrs. Dees, the principal, told me this morning that you would be visiting our school for a few days. I'm so glad to have you in our class. My name is Miss Parker, and I'll be your teacher while you're here." Miss Parker's warm brown eyes looked into Iliana's shining blue eyes. Straightening back up, Miss Parker called out, smiling, "Come on, children, line up straight. Single file and no talking, and keep your hands to yourself." She returned to the sandy haired boy, and taking his hand, led the children to her classroom.

Room I-B was a wonderful place for the first graders. Five round tables with four chairs each sat in a circle around the room, surrounding a large white bathtub on legs, filled with pillows, stuffed animals and puppets. Each corner contained an activity center. In the corner nearest the door were mounds of different colored clay on a low table, with cookie cutters and rolling pins neatly stored in a tray below. By the windows next to the chalkboard were eight easels, each holding a large pad of white paper hung over a row of jars filled with brightly colored paint. In the corner away from the chalkboard was a large braided rug surrounded by low shelves filled with storybooks. In the last corner was another low table filled with scissors, colored papers, glue, feathers, empty toilet paper rolls, beads, and other materials, each pile sorted and labeled carefully. Between the last two corners, in the back of the classroom, sat Miss Parker's desk, cluttered and filled with jars holding pencils and bright red wooden apples with bites taken out of them and yellow and black worms poking their heads out. The children followed Miss Parker and the boy with the sandy hair into the classroom and moved toward the tables. Mara walked straight to the table next to Miss Parker's desk and began slowly walking around it, studying the names taped to the table.

"'Mara!' There I am, right there!" she said pointing and smiling at Iliana. "See? M – a – r – a. Mara!" She took Iliana past the table to a large bright blue cabinet, filled with cubbyholes, each with a name carefully taped on. "'Mara!' See, there I am again!" She carefully placed her backpack on a hook on the back at the cubbyhole, and placed her and Iliana's lunch sacks on the top shelf. Iliana watched her closely, following her back to her chair at the round table.

"Iliana?" Iliana turned to Miss Parker, who was standing by her desk and smiling. "Would you like to get a chair from the craft table to put by Mara?"

Iliana turned to Mara, who was pointing to the corner. "Yes, ma'am." Iliana took the chair and placed it carefully by Mara, who had scooted over next to the sandy haired boy who was sitting beside her.

The second morning bell rung and the children quieted down to hear the morning announcements. "Good morning, children!" the voice from the intercom began, followed by the Pledge of Allegiance and a few announcements, which ended with a reminder for students about the week ending pep rally for the high school football team.

"Okay, children. Take your seats." Miss Parker smiled and cleared her throat as the students noisily slid their chairs out and then back in again under themselves. "This morning, I would like us all to welcome a visitor. Mara, would you like to introduce your friend?"

Mara felt her face flushing, and nervously stood. She led Iliana to the front of Miss Parker's desk. She looked toward Iliana. Seeing her there beside her made her feel comfortable, giving her the strength to begin speaking. "This is my friend, Iliana." She shrugged her shoulders, not knowing what else to say as the other children giggled nervously.

"Well, Iliana, it is a pleasure to have you with us," Miss Parker said, smiling. "Would you like to tell the class a little about yourself?" Miss Parker watched Iliana attentively and bit her lower lip subconsciously, waiting for Iliana's reply. She had observed her carefully, and she did not believe she had ever seen her before. She hoped for some clue about the young girl she could give to Mrs. Dees.

Iliana paused and smiled at Miss Parker, and then turned to the class. "My name is Iliana," she began, shrugging her shoulders in mimic of Mara while turning toward her, "and I am Mara's friend." As the classroom began to quiet, she took Mara's hand and squeezed it gently. Once again, she turned to Miss Parker and smiled, saying nothing else.

Miss Parker smiled back while still biting her lip, wondering if she could prompt Iliana to reveal anything else. She decided to look for help among the children. "Does anyone here have any questions for Iliana? Where she is from, or about her family?" She knew the power of peer pressure, and felt more comfortable letting the children ask than her asking Iliana directly.

The children again began to giggle nervously, and wiggled around on their seats. The boy with the sandy hair finally raised his hand high into the air, elbow locked, with all five of his fingers stretching straight out. "Yes, Duane, what would you like to know?" Miss Parker had just begun to get to know the students, but already could recognize certain individual personality traits. She had hoped that Duane would not be the first to ask, hoping that one of the less silly children would ask first.

"I have a question, Miss Parker," Duane said, with a smile that showed two missing front teeth.

"Yes, Duane, go ahead," Miss Parker encouraged, her smile fading.

"Do you like frogs?" The class giggled louder as Duane nervously put his hands up over his eyes and wiggled his body. Miss Parker couldn't help but to smile at the boy, shaking her head back and forth as she did so. She looked at Iliana, who seemed to be thinking about the answer.

"Yes, I think so," Iliana finally answered with a smile, seemingly confused as to why her answer caused even louder giggles from the class.

"Does someone else have a question?" Miss Parker asked as Duane sat back in his chair, knocking the books out of the bottom as he did so. Leah, a tall pretty girl with a face thick with freckles and long reddish hair, shot her hand straight into the air, holding it high with her other hand leveraged behind her head.

"Do you have any sisters?" Leah had three older brothers, and was the youngest in her family.

Iliana paused, and then smiled, shaking her head. "No, I don't have any sisters, or brothers. Just Mara."

Miss Parker wondered what she meant, deciding that Iliana must have already bonded closely to Mara in the absence of her own family. She felt badly for Iliana and her family, and hoped again that new information would come out of these questions.

"Miss Parker, I have a question," Amy Lynn, a small blonde girl on the front row whispered, holding her hand barely off of the top of her desk.

Miss Parker had already become attached to Amy Lynn, whose mom had died while giving birth to her and was being raised by her dad. Her large brown eyes had a way of looking right through you, and her smile, rare as it was, could melt any heart. Miss Parker smiled and nodded her head encouragingly, and then looked up at the rest of the class, putting her finger to her mouth to quiet their nervous chatter so Amy Lynn's voice could be heard.

"Do you have a Mom?" Amy Lynn asked, her eyes watching Iliana intently. Iliana stood quietly, returning her gaze, and then began walking slowly toward Amy Lynn's desk. She reached out her hand and gently touched her hair, brushing it downward with her fingers, and bent down to eye level with Amy Lynn. Tears began to form in both of the children's eyes as they looked at each other, as though in a trance. The class watched quietly. Even Duane had stopped wiggling as he watched the two girls.

Miss Parker blinked back her own tears as she watched the two silent, still girls, Amy Lynn in her desk, and Iliana leaning in front of her. Through her tears, Miss Parker could see the area surrounding the two girls began to glow with an almost indiscernible soft white light. She blinked back her tears to see more clearly and clenched her jaw, fighting the emotion rising up within her, not wanting the class to see her crying. Iliana reached her hand to Amy Lynn's face, and carefully wiped a tear from her cheek. Miss Parker could see Amy Lynn's lips spread into a smile as the young girl grabbed hold of Iliana's hand. Iliana returned the smile, straightened, and returned to the front of the classroom. Once again she took Mara's hand and stood facing the class, smiling, answering Amy Lynn's question without ever saying a single word. Miss Parker reached for a tissue and wiped her own eyes, wondering if she had seen the halo of light, or if her tears had made the light radiate. The class had remained quiet, peacefully quiet, and Miss Parker made a decision that the questioning was over, that it had served a purpose.

"Thank you, Mara. Thank you, Iliana. We are all delighted to have you visit our class!" The class began a quiet twitter as the two girls returned to their seats, and then once again erupted in giggles as Duane fell out of his desk as he bent over trying to pick up his books.

The rest of the morning class passed happily for the two girls as they spent time at the craft station, making Indian bonnets for each other from cardboard strips and feathers. Amy Lynn had joined the two at the craft table and had spent the morning coloring a red heart she had cut out, carefully spelling out D A D on the front. Despite Duane's distractions, Miss Parker had been able to watch the girls closely, listening in on their conversations. She had heard nothing new that would shed light on Iliana's mystery, nothing but three six year old girls talking about scissors, paste, and crayons.

"Excuse me for the interruption." The voice on the intercom startled the children as they stopped their activities and looked up at the corner of the ceiling where Mrs. Dees's voice was coming from. "There will be a short staff meeting in the lounge during lunch. Please dismiss your classes for lunch ten minutes early and report to the Teachers' Lounge." Miss Parker looked at the clock above the chalkboard, remembering that it had said '9:00' since school had started, and glanced at her own wristwatch.

"Okay, children, time to clean up. We need to get ready for lunch." She felt her own stomach grumble, and hoped that the unscheduled meeting would not last too long. "Come on, boys and girls, line up at the restroom. Paint table first!" The children began to make their way to the door, some stopping to pick up their mess before leaving. Duane began making race car sounds and sped to the front, screeching his brakes before plowing into the closed door. Miss Parker let Duane lead the first group of children across the hall to the restrooms, and watched from the doorway to make sure the boys and girls found the right door. One by one, the groups left and then returned to the classroom, each child returning with a brown paper towel that they threw in the trash basket beside the door.

Finally, the last group returned, and Miss Parker began to line the children at the door, again allowing Duane to lead the line. "Duane, hands at your side, and no running! Okay, boys and girls. Straight line, follow Duane, and no talking!" The children started down the hallway, joining other lines of children making their way to the cafeteria. From the back of the line, Miss Parker could hear the sound of Duane, shifting gears in his imaginary racing car at the front of the line.

The cafeteria was empty when Miss Parker's class entered, with long rows of tables running the length of the room. The children lined up inside the door, their heads not quite reaching the top of the counter beside them. One by one, Miss Parker handed the children a tray with a plate of one chicken drumstick, mashed potatoes, green beans, and canned pears. The children headed to another, lower table, where they were offered the choice of chocolate or white milk, and were handed a fork and napkin. Mara and Iliana, along with a few other children, headed directly to the table, lunch sacks in hand. By the time Miss Parker's class began filling the shortened tables at the back of the cafeteria, the noise from the front had become overwhelming as fifth and sixth graders pushed and shoved in line, and second, third, and fourth graders began making the way to their own tables.

Mara and Iliana opened their lunch sacks and carefully spread the contents. Each had a plastic container filled with cut apples, carrots and raisins, a cheese sandwich carefully wrapped in wax paper and a small thermos filled with fruit juice. Iliana bent her head silently for a moment and then, giving Mara a smile, opened her sandwich and took a bite. She loved the taste of the food, the texture, and the smells. She felt the cheese slip free of the bread in her mouth and crumble as she began to chew, mixing again with the bread between her teeth before falling down her throat. She loved every experience, each sensation, feeling them for the first time, sharing them with Mara. Before, she had watched Mara eat, wondering what the sensation felt like. Taking another bite of the sandwich, Iliana smiled again at Mara, watching as she, too, bit into her sandwich.

"Class?" Miss Parker stood at the head of the low table, clearing her throat. "Please pay attention to the lunch monitors, and enjoy your lunch!" Looking around and spying Duane trying to stick a spoon to his nose, she added, "and please behave!" She gave Duane a long, last look as he removed the spoon from his nose and smiled back at her, showing the gap in his bottom teeth. Miss Parker turned and headed to the cafeteria exit, joining several other teachers along the way. The children watched as Miss Parker left, and then they quickly returned to their lunches.

As they ate their lunches, Duane continued to keep Miss Parker's class laughing, blowing bubbles into a straw until his chocolate milk overflowed the carton and ran onto the table. Even Amy Lynn giggled when he split his Oreo cookie in half and placed each of the brown circles in his eyes, making grunting noises until the lunch monitor spied him and silenced him with a stare. The children finished eating and took turns taking their trays and bags to a large trash can by the door, emptying them carefully and pouring the liquids into a bucket on the floor. The lunch monitor lined them up again and took them out onto the playground, where they quickly headed to their favorite activities, burning up the excess sugar that they had put into their systems.

Mara, Iliana, and Amy Lynn headed toward the merry go round squeaking under the shade of a spreading mesquite tree, and hopped on to the spinning disk. One by one, they took turns pushing with the other children and then jumped back on, holding tightly to the bars leading to the middle. Iliana felt the air rushing through her hair, and laughed as Mara and Amy Lynn tried to make their way to the middle. Iliana joined their struggle, and working together, the three made their way, inch by inch, to the center. The three joined hands and stood, facing each other, watching as their faces stood still against the wildly spinning background of trees, children, and school buildings.

Suddenly, the spinning stopped, almost violently. The three girls toppled over, losing their grip on each other, and tried to focus on the world around them. The background continued to spin, just as before as the children stood still. They viewed trees, school buildings, children, and then Duane; trees, school buildings, children, and then Duane.

"Hey, let go!" One of the children on the edge was pushing Duane, trying to get him to loose his grip on the merry go round. Duane stood, laughing defiantly, enjoying the attention that came from the shouting children that he had stopped by grabbing hold of the bar and digging his feet into the dirt.

Iliana held the bar and made her way to the edge, finally jumping to the ground. Quickly, the earth rose to meet her as her legs gave way, not being able to coordinate the still spinning ground that her eyes still saw with the act of standing upright.

"Unhh," Iliana cried, as she impacted the ground, her head landing on a sharp rock protruding from the ground.

"Iliana!" Mara screamed, jumping down beside her, bending over her carefully. "Iliana! Are you okay?" Iliana raised her hand to her own cheek, and felt warm, damp fluid sticking to her fingers. Fire was burning on the surface of her skin, and the sensation of needles sticking into her skin overwhelmed her. She closed her eyes against the pain, trying to comprehend it, but feeling only the overwhelming sensation on her face was unable to make sense of it.

"It hurts," Iliana said softly, opening her eyes to meet Mara's. She felt her own tears flowing out of her eyes, running to her cheek, mixing with the thick fluid gathering there. Mara carefully brushed back Iliana's hair, and saw the angry, red mark on her face, blood beginning to ooze out from the scrape. Iliana watched as Mara eyes, full of anxiety and compassion, turned into an angry storm, pupils dilating rapidly from the swelling emotion within the small girl. Quickly, Mara rose from Iliana and turned to Duane, her hand clinching into a fist as she turned.

"You hurt her!" Mara cried out, beginning to approach the small boy who was grinning at her, still clutching the bar of the merry go round with his feet dug into the ground. Iliana saw Duane's smile quickly fade from his face, his eyes growing large as his eyebrows shot upward, watching Mara quickly approaching. "You hurt her!" Mara repeated, standing before Duane, beginning to pull her hand back behind her, muscles tensing in her arm.

Through her pain, Iliana watched Mara intently, and watched as her arm reached all the way back, pausing briefly before beginning to move forward. Iliana spoke instinctively, letting her feelings and emotions swirl behind her as she spoke definitively the words that rose from within her.

"No, Mara, don't hit him."

Mara froze, her arm stopping midway towards Duane's nose. She turned to Iliana, still lying on the ground, as Duane took the opportunity to run, tripping over his feet as he hastily made his retreat. Mara stared at Iliana on the ground, mouth slightly open, head cocked slightly. She seemed confused, not understanding what had just happened. "Who said that?"

Iliana looked back at Mara, not certain how to reply.

"I've heard that voice. I've heard it before," Mara continued, looking around for the source of the words, and then looking back again at Iliana. "Iliana, did you say that?"

Iliana looked up at her friend, and slowly touched her cheek. She wondered again if she had been right to have told Mara who she was the night before. It was the first time that she had spoken to Mara like that, the way she spoke before she was trapped. "Mara..." was all that she could say, as she looked away from Mara and down at the ground.

Mara came to Iliana and sat beside her as the other children once again began pushing the merry go round; all except Amy Lynn, who joined the two girls on the ground. "I don't like him." Amy Lynn watched Duane from across the playground, where he sat by himself throwing rocks against the back of the classroom. "He's a show off!"

♦

"Okay, class, settle down!" Miss Parker looked over the classroom at the children who were still full of energy from lunch and the playground. "Everyone, in your seats." She looked around at the students, and saw Iliana holding a paper towel to her face. "Iliana, what happened?" Miss Parker moved to the table in front of her and bent down to eye level with Iliana, putting her fingers out to her damp cheek.

"Duane made her fall!" shouted Amy Lynn, surprising Miss Parker.

"Did not! Did not!" Duane shouted, wiggling his hips and sticking his thumbs in his ears, waving his hands back and forth.

"He did, too, Miss Parker. He made the merry go round stop, and Iliana fell off and got hurt!" Amy Lynn's face was red, and she looked almost on the verge of tears.

"Did not! Did not!" Duane continued, becoming more vigorous in his movements.

"Duane!" Miss Parker's raised voice stopped the boy in his tracks, and he slowly sank back into his seat. She continued to glare at him until he was fully seated and quiet, and then turned her attention back to Iliana.

"Let's have a look, Iliana. Oh, my, that's a nasty scrape." She carefully touched the area around the scrape, watching for Iliana's reaction. The scrape was bright red, but it appeared to be only superficial. "Are you okay?"

"Yes, Ma'am. It's not too bad, I don't think." Iliana responded to Miss Parker's kindness and tried to reassure her, but felt the pain still burning her face, and wondered how long it would last. Pain was an experience, she thought, which she could live without, if that was possible.

"Duane did it, Miss Parker, I saw him." Mara spoke out. Miss Parker turned to her, and saw her watching Iliana. "I was gonna hit him, but Iliana told me not to."

Miss Parker smiled in disbelief, shaking her head. She loved teaching first graders; their innocence and honesty always amazed her. She was glad to be back teaching after the long summer, and thought that this class would be an interesting one. "I'm glad you didn't, Mara. I'll deal with Duane later." Miss Parker smiled at Mara and patted her hand, and slowly straightened out to address the class.

"Class, Mrs. Dees, our principal, announced that yesterday there had been an accident in front of the school. Some of you may have seen it." She looked out over the class, making sure of eye contact before continuing. "A large truck carrying some chemicals turned over in front of the school, and spilled some of the chemicals out onto the road. Mrs. Dees says that everything is okay, but they're going to have to shut down the school for the afternoon, and maybe tomorrow while they clean up the chemicals." Miss Parker wondered if the children understood the word 'chemicals', but decided that it sounded better than uranium, or radioactive materials – those were the words that Mrs. Dees had used telling the staff. She wondered if the words sounded as frightening to the children as they had to her. "We've already started calling your parents, and they will be coming soon to pick you up." She paused and looked over the class again, watching for signs of anxiety. "I've got a paper for you to take home to your parents that explains what happened. Amy Lynn? Would you please pass these out to each student?" She considered letting the students ask questions so that she could reassure them, but looking at Duane, decided against it. She felt that the parents could address their children's anxieties and questions, knowing that Mrs. Dees could explain the situation to the parents, leaving her out of the loop, at least for now. She released the students to the activity centers again while they waited for their parents to come to pick them up.

One by one, the parents came, and took their child from Miss Parker's class, reading over the note and asking whispered questions.

Micah was one of the first to arrive, having been home when the call came. She and Aaron walked in with Luke Johnson, Amy Lynn's dad, and quietly knocked on the door. "Miss Parker?" Micah said softly, entering the room. "I'm Mara's mom – I'm here to pick up Mara and Iliana. Is everything okay?"

"Hi, Mrs. Summers; come on in Mr. Johnson. Amy Lynn, Mara, Iliana, get your backpacks. Your parents are here." Miss Parker answered Micah's and Luke's questions about the early release, explaining that the State Natural Resource Commission had asked Mrs. Dees to close the school while the uranium company cleaned up the spill that had occurred the day before. She assured them that the kids were safe, that no one believed that they had been exposed to any dangerous levels of radioactivity, but that everyone had decided to be extra cautious, considering what had happened. She said that Mrs. Dees felt that school would be closed only that afternoon and the next day, but that they should keep an eye out for local announcements if it would take longer. Besides, she said, there was a little tropical storm moving up out of the Gulf, and at last they were predicting some rain for the area. The kids could take the unexpected vacation day and enjoy one last day of summer, splashing in the rain. Miss Parker said that she hoped that it would not be an inconvenience, and agreed with Mrs. Dees that it was in the best interest of the children.

"I'm sure everything will be fine, Miss Parker. I work out at the mine, and these guys know what they are doing." Tall and deeply tanned, Luke Johnson wore a starched khaki shirt and jeans and wore a white golf cap. He had an easy smile and light brown eyes that peered through premature wrinkles coming from the corners, betraying his long days of working in the sun. "I feel real bad about what happened, but I'm sure that the crew will have it cleaned up in no time. How are the kids taking it?" Amy Lynn had run up with her backpack on and wrapped herself around her dad's leg. Looking up, her face lit up in a smile.

"Oh, they're doing fine. I told them what happened in very simple terms, but I don't think they really understood any of it – except that they get out early! Anyway, it's still so early in the year. They're not used to the routine yet, so this wasn't disruptive for them at all." Miss Parker liked Luke Johnson, and had she not already been engaged to be married, would have encouraged him to continue the conversation. She couldn't help but be attracted to his broad shoulders and pleasant face. It was hard not to give a little flirtatious smile, and catching herself, she blushed slightly.

Luke noticed the smile and the blush, and he grinned back slightly. "Well, Miss Parker, we better be going. Just let me know if there's anything the company can do to help. Hey, maybe later on in the year, ya'll can come out for a tour! Amy Lynn would love to show off where her daddy works to the rest of the class, right Amy Lynn?"

Amy Lynn's face shined brightly, looking at her dad as she answered "OK!" and took his hand, pushing a piece of red construction paper in the shape of a heart up to his face.

"Miss Parker, how are the girls?" Micah's smile turned to a look of concern as she saw Iliana approaching, her face still red from the scrape. "Oh, my. Iliana, are you okay? What happened?" Micah turned from Iliana to Miss Parker, waiting for an explanation.

"Duane made her fall!" Amy Lynn called out from the door, turning to wave as she left with her dad.

"It's all right, Mrs. Summers. It was just a playground accident. I think the girls cleaned it up before they came back from lunch, and it looks fine to me, but you probably ought to put some antibiotic ointment on it when you get home." Miss Parker watched Micah closely, trying to judge what kind of parent she was. Mara seemed so happy today, with Iliana, but had been so moody the day before. She had heard the rumors going around town about the Summers family, but had always made it a habit to reserve judgment for herself. She watched as Micah bent down to Iliana and gently looked at her cheek, and then reached over and gave Mara a hug. Both children seemed happy to see her, and Miss Parker quickly decided that Micah cared for the children. Lord knew she had seen enough kids whose parents didn't seem to care at all.

"She's okay, Mom. Duane made her fall off of the merry go round. I was gonna take care of Duane, but Iliana told me not to. I was gonna clobber him!" Mara took her fist and pounded it into her hand for emphasis.

"Oh, no, Mara." Micah looked surprised at her daughter's aggressiveness, and glanced up embarrassedly at Miss Parker to view her reaction.

"It's all right, Mrs. Summers," laughed Miss Parker. "Nobody got 'clobbered', and everything has been taken care of. I don't think Duane deliberately hurt her. He's just kind of...active."

"Well, okay then. As long as nobody's getting clobbered, I guess we'll all live." Micah gave Mara a mock threatening look, and straightened up to Miss Parker. "Miss Parker, could I talk to you for just a minute?"

Miss Parker looked at Micah's face briefly, and then turned to the girls. "Mara? Iliana? Would you two mind picking up the activity center for me for just a minute? Look at that big mess at the clay center. Could you help put the clay away for me?"

The two girls said 'yes' and hurried to the table while Miss Parker found chairs for Micah and Aaron. "Did Iliana say anything? Anything, about her family, or anything?"

"No, Mrs. Summers, nothing at all. I introduced her to the class, and they asked her questions about herself, but she didn't volunteer anything." Miss Parker looked at Micah as Micah turned to watch the two girls cleaning up the table, and could sense the concern in her. "Mrs. Dees told me that your kids just found her at your house, that she just wandered up. You don't have any idea who she is, or where she came from?"

"No, nothing at all. I've tried to find out; the sheriff's tried to find out. We were hoping that maybe someone from here at school would recognize her. I don't know what to do." Micah turned back to Miss Parker, and decided to confide in her. "I just don't want them to take her and put her in some foster home, or something. She is so sweet, and she seems to be happy staying with us. I just hate to think of her being upset anymore than I know she already is."

"I know. She is just the sweetest thing, isn't she?" Miss Parker looked carefully at Micah, and decided that she could be trusted. "You know, Mrs. Summers, this might sound crazy, but maybe this is something. Today, one of the little girls, Amy Lynn — she was the one who just left with her dad — asked Iliana if she had a mom. Amy Lynn's mom died when Amy was born. Iliana didn't say a word. She just walked up to her, and touched her, and both of them started to cry. It was really something, like, special, you know?" Miss Parker looked again at Micah, wondering if she should continue. "I don't know if it was my imagination, or what, but it seemed like the air all around the two of them just started to glow. I never saw anything like it." Miss Parker could feel the hairs on the back of her neck begin to rise, sending small shivers down her back. "Maybe it means something. Maybe it means I'm going crazy!" Miss Parker laughed nervously, "but somehow the two of them connected. Do you know what I mean? I mean, maybe they share something, like both of their mammas are dead or something — I don't know." Miss Parker looked over at the two girls. "Maybe I am going crazy," she said softly, shaking her head slowly.

Micah looked at Miss Parker and then back at the girls. She, too, had sensed something different about Iliana, something special. She had tried to put it out of her mind, focusing instead on finding her family, but there was something — something she didn't understand. No, she didn't think that Miss Parker was crazy, but she didn't have any idea what this was all about. She turned back to Miss Parker. "I believe you. I don't know what you saw, but I believe you. There is something special about that little girl. I just don't have any idea what it is."

"Well, I hope you find out soon, for her sake – and for yours," Miss Parker smiled, rising from her chair to escort Micah, Aaron, Mara, and Iliana from the room.

Inez

Micah noticed the clouds forming thin wisps high overhead as she drove back to the farmhouse. As she stopped the car and began to unload the kids, she felt the air moving from out of the north, pushing the overhead clouds southward, spiraling around a center point somewhere out to the southeast. The air felt cooler, bringing with it the faint smell of coming rain, but at the same time the dropping pressure made her feel uneasy. As she got out of the car, she looked upward, and thought the clouds in the sky looked as though they were a giant swirl moving across the afternoon sun.

"Come on, kids. In the house," Micah called out.

Ben unbuckled Aaron from the middle of the front seat and both boys jumped out of the front passenger door and raced toward the house. Mara and Iliana stayed in the back seat a few moments, and then each opened their own door and got out, joining together again at the back of the car.

"Please, Mom? Can Iliana and I play outside for a little while?" Mara pleaded, trying to persuade her mother.

"Yes, Mara, but first I want you both out of those school clothes. Find some of your old clothes for Iliana to play in. Hurry!" Micah scooted her hand behind the girls, herding them toward the house. Micah wasn't sure how much longer Iliana would be staying and wanted to be sure that the two girls didn't run out of school clothes before she had a chance to do laundry. She glanced up at the sky one last time before she joined the children in the house.

Ben and Aaron were at the kitchen table, each holding a butter knife in their hand. A jar of peanut butter sat between them, and bread was spread out on the table next to a jar of grape jelly. "First you put the peanut butter on the bread, and then you put the jelly on the other bread," Ben was saying.

Aaron listened intently; watching as his brother carefully dug into jar with the knife and then began spreading the thick brown goo on a slice of bread. "First – pea – nut – butter," Aaron said, trying to copy his brother's actions, digging his own knife deep into the jar, gathering up the peanut butter on the knife, his knuckles and his wrist. Mara and Iliana had disappeared up the stairs and were making small, soft footsteps down the hallway.

"Hurricane Inez was downgraded this morning to a tropical storm as it made landfall on the Texas coast, thrashing the coastal village of Port O'Connor with 90 mile per hour winds and high tides." Micah turned her attention to the television that she had left on in her rush to get the kids from school. A woman in a bright yellow rain coat peered from the screen, rain dripping from her hat as she clutched a microphone. "The storm struck with a fury early this morning, unleashing torrential rains and hurricane force winds, with gusts up to 110 miles per hour as it battered this isolated town on the Texas coast. Residents who had not evacuated woke this morning to a storm tide that prevented them from leaving on the only road leading from town. Water quickly rising into their homes forced many to seek emergency shelter." Micah watched as the screen showed a group huddled together in a school cafeteria, and then switched to flooded streets and homes. "Fortunately, there were no fatalities, and only a few minor injuries. Inez, now a tropical storm with maximum winds of 50 miles per hour, has begun to move inland from the coast, leaving the residents to clean up in her aftermath." Micah watched as the screen returned to newsmen sitting at a studio desk, and turned her attention back to the kitchen table.

"Aaron, no!" Micah rushed toward the young boy as he turned the jelly jar upside down over his face, looking inside at the purple jelly. A giant glob was poised on the lip of the jar, gathering weight as it began a surge from the jar to Aaron's face. Micah made it almost in time, grabbing the jar from his hand and turning it upright, but not before the glob had broken free and landed squarely on Aaron, covering most of the area between his eyes and mouth. "Why did you do that, Aaron?" Micah asked, struggling between being amused and upset at Aaron's surprised look as he began wiping the jelly with the back of his hand.

"Ben – do – it," Aaron protested, looking at his brother staring up into the jar of peanut butter, scraping the bottom with a knife, trying to get out the last of it. Ben looked over at Aaron, and seeing the growing mess, quickly brought the peanut butter jar down and removed the knife.

Micah reached to the sink to grab a dish cloth to begin wiping Aaron's face, and as she did, she saw the sheriff's patrol car turn into the drive, windshield wipers on. She noticed the absence of the ever present cloud of dust behind the car. Micah could see a fine mist beginning to fall, even though the sun continued to shine. "Come here, Aaron, let me clean your face," she said, still looking out the window at the approaching car. She reached down to lift Aaron to the counter, and as she did so, felt her hand grow sticky with peanut butter as she grabbed his. "Oh, honey..." she said, as she began cleaning his hand, becoming frustrated with the growing mess and the car already stopped outside.

"It – not – honey. It – pea – nut – butter!" Aaron said, smiling at his mom.

Micah's attention returned to the boy for just a moment, returning his smile. Aaron always had the knack of bringing Micah back to the little joys, the things that got her through the obstacles of each day. She tweaked his nose with the dishcloth, satisfied that his face was clean enough, and put him back down on the floor. Drying her own hands, she went to the door to greet the sheriff. She heard him scraping his heavy boots on the porch's uneven wood, and opened the door. His hand was already raised to knock on the door, and he seemed surprised that the door opened prematurely.

"Hi, Sheriff!" Micah was genuinely happy to see his now familiar face, in spite of the circumstances. He was, in fact, the only visitor other than the mailman that Micah had since moving out to the farmhouse, and Micah welcomed the company.

The sheriff looked down at his boots, wiping them one more time and checking the board for signs of remaining mud. "Looks like it's getting ready to rain out here. It's already coming down in town," the sheriff said, looking around behind him. Micah felt the cool mist on her face, and noticed the sky growing darker, giving the farm an unnatural look for the middle of the day. "Mind if I come on in?" the sheriff asked, taking his hat from his head and trying to straighten out his hair with his fingers.

"Sure, Sheriff. I'm sorry. Come on in out of the rain." Micah saw large drops beginning to fall from the edge of the tin roof, carrying thick, brown liquid down toward the dry ground. The wind was beginning to blow harder in gusts from the north, driving the heavy brown drops up onto the porch where they landed in the dust.

"Okay, Mom, all dressed!" Mara and Iliana came running down the stairs, dressed in jeans and tee shirts, Iliana's faded with the words 'Sea World' written over a jumping porpoise. They stopped suddenly as they entered the kitchen, seeing the sheriff standing on the porch.

"Hey, kids, come say 'hi' to the sheriff." Micah brought each of the girls under an arm as she stepped back, allowing the sheriff to step up into the kitchen.

"Why, hello, little ladies! Hi there, Iliana," the sheriff greeted, bending his knees and squeezing his ample gut onto his belt, coming to eye level with the girls. He carefully put out one hand on the floor to balance himself, and pulled his hat onto his knees. "How's Miss Parker treatin' you out at Hondo Elementary?"

Iliana smiled at the imposing figure, just inches in front of her face, and pulled back slightly in Micah's arm. "I like Miss Parker," Iliana said quietly, and her smile grew bigger.

"Well, Iliana, how about Mrs. Summers here, and her family. Everyone treatin' you okay here?" the sheriff asked, looking up at Micah and smiling.

"Oh, yes sir! They are very nice to me!" Iliana said, continuing to look directly at the sheriff, happy that at last he had learned her name.

"Well, that's good, real good, Iliana. You'll let me know if they start being mean, you hear?" the sheriff said, pushing up with his hand and straightening up, towering over the children and Micah. "Where you two headin' to now?"

Mara looked from the sheriff to Micah and answered, "Mom, can we go outside to play? We heard the rain hitting the window. Can we please go outside, please?"

Micah looked down at Mara, and felt the cool breeze blowing in the front door, bringing with it the smell of the falling rain. She, too, felt the urge to run outside and play in the rain, to feel the drops fall on her face and mud gush up between her toes. "Okay, I guess. But get the raincoats on. I put them in the closet under the stairs – I don't want you getting soaked. And look in the box on the floor for your rubber boots. I think your old pair might fit Iliana."

"Yes, yes! Thanks Mom, I love you!" Mara called out, already heading to the closet. "Come on, Iliana, I told you she'd say okay!" Iliana smiled again at the sheriff and followed Mara towards the closet.

"Me – too, – Mom? Can – I – go – too?" Aaron looked up at his mom, imploring with his large brown eyes.

Micah looked down and smiled. "Ben, do you want to take your brother out in the rain? Lord knows when you'll get the chance again."

"Sure thing, Mom!" Ben swept Aaron up from the floor and carried him toward the closet where the girls were rummaging through a box.

Micah watched as the children slipped into bright yellow plastic coats and pulled up black rubber boots, stacking their own shoes neatly against the wall. Micah turned back to the sheriff and asked, "Sheriff, why don't you come in and sit down? Let me get you a drink of ice tea."

"Thank you, Mrs. Summers, that would be nice." He stepped forward out of the doorway just in time to avoid the children rushing to the door, umbrellas in hand.

"Ben, you make sure that everyone's okay out there. I don't want anyone blowing away!" Micah hollered out to the back porch, watching the kids push out against the blowing rain.

"Sure, Mom!" Ben yelled back. Aaron found a small button on his umbrella and pushed it, watching the green golfing umbrella that his dad had left behind explode out with a loud popping sound. He held it tightly against the rain, pushing out against the wind as he stepped off the porch. Ben opened his own umbrella, and stepped down with his little brother into the puddle at the bottom of the step, splashing the water as he stepped. "We'll be careful!"

Micah watched through the kitchen window as the two girls followed the boys from the porch, laughing and splashing in the rain. She pulled the pitcher out of the refrigerator and poured the tea over two glasses of ice. "Sheriff, do you like sugar?" she called out to the dining table where the sheriff had made himself comfortable.

"Yes, ma'am," the sheriff answered, "three spoonfuls, if you don't mind."

Micah reached for the sugar and added two spoonfuls, and then put the spoon back into the sugar bowl and added just a tiny bit more, hoping that it would be enough to satisfy the sheriff. She reached into a small cup on the counter and opened a pink bag of sweetener for herself, adding half of the bag to her own glass, and carefully folding the bag and returning it to the cup. "Here you go, Sheriff. Ice cold tea." Micah pulled out a chair and sat down, joining the sheriff at the table. She picked up a blue napkin and carefully wiped some peanut butter that was smeared on the table in front of the sheriff.

"Thank you, Mrs. Summers," the sheriff said, pushing his chair under the table just a little more, toward Micah. He took a long drink of his tea and then set the glass down, swirling the ice and tea as he did so, trying to dissolve the sugar still remaining in the bottom of the glass. "How's Iliana doing. Is she opening up to you at all?"

Micah looked at the sheriff, and thought about her answer. "Well, she's really adjusted to being here. I mean, she seems happy and everything. She hasn't cried at all today, and Miss Parker thought she did okay at school. She did get a small bump on her head, something about, Duane — I think that's his name. Pushing her down, something to do with the merry go round. She seems okay; Miss Parker thought it was very minor." Micah looked at the sheriff and realized that she had gone on without answering his question. He sat patiently across from her, waiting for her to continue. Micah smiled, and after a moment, continued. "I don't know, Sheriff, she hasn't really said anything. I mean, about her family at all. She seems happy enough. I don't know if she just doesn't want to talk about it, or if she really doesn't know." She stopped and looked at the sheriff again, waiting this time for him to respond.

"Well, I don't know what to do," he said after waiting several moments to see if Micah had anything else to offer. He reached out for his tea, and after swirling it around a few more times, put the glass to his mouth and finished drinking the liquid, holding back a piece of ice in his mouth as he put the glass down. He looked out the still open kitchen door where he could see the kids splashing in the rain, and slowly chewed the ice cube. "I've checked everywhere, and nobody seems to know nothing. There's no one with her description reported missing anywhere in the state, and we're checking the national files to see what we come up with." He turned back to Micah and swallowed the last of the ice cube. "I know there's gonna be a truck load of kids looking just like her missing, and I guess we'll have to go through each one of those reports to see if she matches up. I just wish we had something, anything to go on." He looked back at the children and added, "Somebody somewhere has to be worried sick about that kid."

Micah turned her gaze away from the sheriff and joined him in looking out the back door. The rain ran off from the corrugated tin roof, streams running down evenly spaced out through which she could see the random pattern of drops falling from the sky. The rain was coming straight down now in a steady downpour, filling the potholes in the driveway with puddles, attracting the children as they splashed about. Iliana held Mara's hand as the two stood carefully by the largest puddle, watching Aaron and Ben splash with their boots through the deepest water. The sound of the rain on the roof, even from downstairs, was loud, drowning out the sounds of the children, but it was easy to imagine their sounds of delight. For a brief moment, Micah longed to be with the children, to join them in their pursuit of pleasure, worrying about nothing. "Yes, Sheriff, you're right. Somebody's worried sick about Iliana right now."

The sheriff looked back at Micah, and bringing the glass to his mouth, put the last piece of ice between his back teeth. "Well, Mrs. Summers, you take good care of that little angel till we find out who she is, if that's still all right with you," the sheriff said, sliding his chair out and standing up, moving the ice to the other side of his mouth and crunching it between his teeth.

"Of course, Sheriff. We'll do the best we can." Micah stood and began walking the sheriff toward the door, listening to him loudly chew the ice as they walked.

The sheriff paused at the doorway, carefully placed his hat on his head and reached into his pocket for the keys to his car. The rain continued falling steadily as he stood there, waiting to see if there was going to be a let up so that he could make his way without getting any wetter than necessary.

"Do you want to borrow an umbrella?" Micah asked, wondering if there were any left in the closet, or if the children had them all.

"No Ma'am, that's all right. A little water never hurt anything." The sheriff looked up towards the sky, and seeing nothing that would indicate a letting up of the rain, put his head down and stepped off the porch. "Good day, Mrs. Summers!" he called out, and made his way quickly to the car. Micah stood and watched as he drove off, splashing the kids to their delight as he drove down the driveway through the puddles.

"Don't get too muddy out there!" Micah called into the rain, knowing full well that the kids couldn't hear her, but feeling better about trying to warn them anyway. She stood there a few minutes longer, watching the sheriff turn out on the road back toward Hondo. The car stopped briefly as a truck pulled out from the hunting camp, the back covered with a tarp. The hunter's car brakes locked the rear tires as they slid in the mud, coming to a rest halfway out onto the highway. Micah could see the sheriff through the beating windshield wipers wave the truck to go on ahead, and she watched as both vehicles headed down the road toward Hondo. Micah stayed a few more minutes on the porch, enjoying the feel of the rain in the air, and then turned to disappear into the kitchen.

Ditto

"Aaron!" Ben yelled, "Come back!"

The small boy in the yellow raincoat was disappearing from view as he turned behind the house. Aaron walked purposefully, having left the other three children playing in the puddles in the road without a word.

"Come on, Mara, Iliana, we gotta go get him," Ben called out.

The three braced themselves against the wind that was once again beginning to pick up, and wished for the umbrellas that they had earlier placed on the back porch. Their clothes had become soaked, even though they wore raincoats, with water seeping up from their water filled boots and dripping down from their rain soaked heads. The hot summer day had turned chilly with the rain, and Ben could feel his teeth chattering in the rain. He passed by the tire swing, already filled with water, as he turned the corner of the house. There, he could see his little brother reaching up high, trying to unlatch the door to the chicken coop. "Come on, Aaron, Mom says we gotta go in!"

"No – go – in!" Aaron said through his teeth, clenched against his own chattering. "Save – baby – chickens!"

Ben reached his brother, and looking into the chicken pen, could see his brother's concern. He didn't know how Aaron could have known, but the chicken pen was indeed beginning to fill with water.

Aaron had managed to reach the latch, and opening the door, had entered into the pen, sloshing through the dirty brown water mixed with floating hay. "Get – eggs! They – all – wet!" he ordered, as he made his way to the back of the pen.

Ben looked down at the ugly water, and taking a breath, entered the pen, seeing several eggs barely visible under the water. "Mara! Iliana! Pick up the eggs!" Ben ordered, "I'm gonna try to help Aaron!" Ben followed Aaron into the back of the pen and ducked low to get under the coop. Bending down, he could see Aaron trying to pick up a chicken from the ground, sitting on a wet mass of straw amidst the rising water. Aaron's arms reached out to the bird, staying steady as the chicken struck out to peck his arms through the raincoat. "Careful, Aaron. It'll bite you!" Ben warned, seeing the angry bird strike out again and again.

"Save – chickens. They – all – wet!" Aaron cried out, finally wrapping his arms around the flapping bird. Ben tried to get closer to help, but moved back away from the frantically flapping bird. Water and feathers sprayed his face as the chicken struggled in Aaron's arms, beating him around his face. Steadily, Aaron lifted the chicken to the shelf, setting it between the other clucking birds already there.

"It's okay, Aaron!" Ben yelled out. "They can fly – they won't drown!"

"Save — chickens! They — drown!" Aaron continued, bending back down to the nest.

Ben saw Aaron reach down to the matted straw and put his hands around something yellow, gathering it up to his chest. Moving forward, he could see ten more of the yellow balls of fuzz huddled together among a pile of broken shells, soaking from the wet straw.

"Help, — Ben! Save — chickens!" Aaron cried out, now frantically.

Ben looked at Aaron, wondering how he knew, and then quickly went to work helping his brother. He tried picking up several of the birds, but was unable to hold more than two of them at a time. Ben watched as Aaron sat down in the mud, trying to gather as many baby chickens as he could in his lap, but they kept hopping out as fast as he could put them in. Suddenly, Ben felt the mother hen shake her feathers, flinging water onto his hair. Looking up at the angry bird Ben saw an open box with dry hay sitting in the corner of the shelf. "Aaron! In the box!" Ben hollered over the cackling birds, pointing at the dry box.

"O — kay!" Aaron answered, carefully standing and lifting the chicks up to the box. Ben caught the soaking babies, and one by one, handed them to Aaron to put in the box. Finally, all of the babies had been lifted to safety and stood in the box, shaking themselves free of the moisture. Aaron stood back and wiped his hands together, looking at the mother chicken still angrily clucking. "It's — o — kay!" Aaron hollered at the bird, stepping back as the hen walked over to the box, looking at the wet chicks. The hen stepped carefully into the box of dry hay and ruffled her body feathers, slowly letting them settle over the peeping chicks as she lowered her body. Over the sound of the rain hitting the metal roof, Aaron and Ben could hear the chick's peeping take less urgent tones, quieting until they could not be heard over the gentle clucking of the mother hen. Aaron looked over at Ben and smiled, "Thank — you, — Ben," and turned to leave the birds.

Entering the outer coop area, they joined Mara and Iliana, each holding an egg in each hand. "I think we found them all. There were only four," Mara hollered into the rain.

Ben again felt the chill of the rain pouring down his neck and shivered against the cold. "Come on, let's go. Mom said we need to get inside!" He reached for the door and opened it, leading the other three children out of the pen. Mara and Iliana carefully carried the eggs, trying to protect them from the falling rain.

"What's that?" Mara yelled out, stopping suddenly outside the door.

"Come on, let's go!" Ben again hollered, lowering his head into the driving rain.

"No, wait! I hear something!" Mara turned to look back in the pen, and started to unlatch the door again, shifting two of the eggs into her free hand.

"Come on! It's just the chickens!" Ben again ordered, moving back to block Mara's entry. He reached out to take his sister's arm, and pushed against the door with his other hand. As he did, he too heard the noise, a high whining coming from the back of the pen. "What is that?" he asked, turning to Mara.

"Look!" Mara yelled out, pointing to a straight white tail sticking out just past the back of the pen. She quickly shoved her two eggs into Ben's hand and headed around the pen to the back. As she neared the back, she could clearly make out the sound of the high pitched whining getting louder and louder. Rounding the corner, Mara froze in her tracks, and braced herself against the impact of Ben right behind her. Ben watched as she slowly bent down, putting her hands out in front of her.

"Hey, boy. Come here, boy," Mara said softly, reaching carefully behind the pen. She put one hand on the animal's head, gently stroking it while she slid the other under its belly, cradling it in her arms as it continued to softly whimper. She turned to her brother and spoke quietly, barely above the rain, "Look, Ben. A puppy."

Mara carefully picked up the soaking puppy, who continued to whimper in her arms. Water dripped from his drooping tail, hanging loosely from an all white body marked by two symmetrical black spots; one over his shoulders and the other over his hips. Water ran off of the tin roof, pouring down Mara's head as she tried to cover the animal, filling the back of her raincoat with water as she bent over. The puppy tried to squirm free in Mara's arms, but finally lay his head quietly on her arm, exhausted from the rain. Ben slowly put his free hand out to pet the puppy's head and stood in the downpour stroking it gently.

"What — is — it?" Aaron made his way to the back of the pen with Iliana, trying to peek around his brother's shoulder at Mara. "Aww, — it — a — puppy!" Aaron said loudly against the sound of the rain hitting the tin roof, putting his hand out to join Ben's on the puppy's head.

Ben glanced up at Aaron and saw Iliana standing quietly behind him, arms folded against the water and wind. "Iliana, look!" Ben moved closer to the wall of the chicken pen, leaving room between him and Aaron for Iliana to squeeze in.

Iliana looked at the puppy and at Mara bent over, trying to protect the puppy from the rain. She wanted to wrap both of them in her arms and shield them from the downpour, protecting them from the rain and cold.

"Come on! We gotta tell Mom!" Mara suddenly straightened and wrapped the puppy tightly in her arms. Standing, she felt the water pour down her back to her waist, and shivered with the cold. She quickly left toward the house, leaving the other children to follow. Ben rushed ahead to the porch and opened the door to the house, trying to shake some of the water off before entering.

"Whoa, there. Off with the boots!" Micah greeted him at the door, blocking his way from entering any farther. Micah saw Mara step up onto the porch with Aaron and Iliana on each side, cradling something white and black in her arms. "Oh, my God. What is it?" she spoke, forgetting about the water and moving Ben into the house to make room for the trio.

The three children solemnly moved into the kitchen, water dripping from their boots and raincoats. Mara carefully unfolded her arms, revealing the puppy that had snuggled quietly. Its eyes looked up at Micah as its head pushed harder into Mara's arms. The children stood quietly as Micah bent down to the puppy's level, putting her hand out slowly to its head. She crouched in front of the children with Ben at her side as the water puddled onto the floor, quietly stroking the small puppy's head.

"Can I keep him, Mom?" Micah looked up from the pup's eyes to Mara's eyes, and marveled at the similarity at that moment, both pleadingly asking for comfort.

Micah looked at Mara and smiled, and looked back down at the soaked animal. "Where did you find it?" she asked, stroking the puppy's back, squeezing water drops from its fur.

"It was behind the chicken pen, Mom. It doesn't have a home, or anything. Can we keep it, please?" Mara asked, sensing her mom's weakened will, trying to take advantage of the moment.

"My word, what were you kid's doing down at the chicken pen?" Micah looked back at Ben. She had told him to come straight into the house, and wondered why they had drifted back to the pen. The pen was on the back of the property, near the ravine that led to the hunting cabin, and Micah was concerned with the kids playing near the filling creek. Though the creek was normally dry, she suspected that it could sometimes hold water during a heavy rain.

Ben shrugged his shoulders and glanced down at the eggs still in his hands. Trying to cover the evidence, he looked to Aaron, hoping to be bailed out of the responsibility that his mom now questioned.

"Ben – help – save – baby – chickens," Aaron said, mimicking his older brother's shrugging shoulders in an exaggerated way.

Micah looked over to Aaron and smiled again, shaking her head slowly. She knew how much Aaron loved his chickens and had waited for the eggs to hatch under the sitting hen. She had also thought about them in the rain, but had dismissed their plight in her concern for her children. Looking at Aaron, she was proud that he had overlooked his own comfort to save the lives of the chicks.

"Please, Mom? I'll take good care of him, I promise!" Mara pleaded, turning Micah's attention back to the little girl.

"Mara, I don't know. I'm sure he belongs to someone," Micah said, wondering where the puppy had come from. "Someone may be out looking for him right now. I don't know if we can keep him or not."

"Like Iliana, Mom." Micah looked back at Ben, wondering what he meant. "We found her, and she's staying here. Nobody came and got her yet." Ben suddenly blushed, looking uncomfortably at Iliana, realizing that his logic may have caused Iliana to feel pain.

Micah saw the embarrassment, and feeling it herself for her son, pulled him and Iliana both toward her, holding them tightly against her, hoping to ease both of their discomfort.

"Okay, we'll keep it." Micah watched as the pleading eyes turned to surprise. "Just like Iliana, until its mom comes for him!" Micah laughed softly, trying to turn the embarrassing moment into a less painful one.

"Thank you, Mom! I promise to take good care of it!" Mara brought the pup up tight against her, giving it a hug. "Come on, Iliana, let's take him to our room to play with him!"

"Hold on, just one minute." Micah stood and felt the wetness where Ben and Iliana had been pulled up against her, and surveyed the growing mess in the kitchen, thinking that it should be contained. "The puppy stays here, by the back door. You can get a towel from upstairs and put it in that box in the laundry room and make it a little bed, but no upstairs!" Micah watched as the kids began to shift to move to her orders, and then hollered, "Stop! Everyone. Boots off, and hang your raincoats on the chair in the corner! I don't want any more mess!" Micah bent and carefully took the puppy from Mara so that Mara could follow her directions. Mara carefully handed the pup to Micah as it once again began wiggling and whining. Micah brought the pup close to her and pet its head, calming the animal. She felt it shivering against her as it tried to snuggle its head into the crook of her arm, and she smiled.

◆

"Petey!" Ben yelled out. He wiggled a piece of string under the puppy's nose, watching it as it playfully jumped on it and tugged.

"No — like — Petey!" Aaron said emphatically, watching the puppy play.

"Petey is a great name, Aaron," Ben replied, "Look at him. Doesn't he look like a Petey?"

"Petey is a bird's name!" Mara said, causing Iliana to giggle behind her. Mara sat on the floor, gently pulling on the puppy's tail as it wiggled back and forth, watching as it occasionally turned to playfully snap and growl at her fingers. "He's definitely not a Petey."

"Okay, how about Pluto?" Ben asked, wishing that he had been allowed the responsibility of naming the pup. 'It's everyone's pup, but Mara gets to name him because she found it,' Micah had instructed, much to the dismay of Ben. He had always wanted a dog, but until now, they had never been allowed one. It didn't seem fair that now Mara got to name him.

"Pluto! That's a planet. No way!" Mara said, making Iliana giggle even harder. "We have to come up with a perfect name, because he's such a cute puppy!" Mara was enjoying her veto power, and seemed contented to spend the afternoon watching Ben grow more and more frustrated. For the first time that Ben could remember, Aaron seemed content to agree with whatever Mara said instead of coming to his defense. Iliana leaned back against the wall, watching and enjoying the activity.

Ben had just about run out of any names that he thought were appropriate for a dog, and was just about to resign himself to living with a dog that his sister would name when, seeing the two identical black spots on the puppy's back, had an inspiration. "Ditto!" The pup looked up and came running to Ben, jumping into his lap.

Mara watched as the puppy jumped up and licked Ben's face. "Ditto?" she wondered aloud, and suddenly the puppy turned and ran back to her, almost knocking her over as he jumped up onto her. Giggling from the floor as the dog licked her face, she repeated the word, "Ditto." The dog began licking more excitedly at the sound of the name, and jumped up and down. "I think he likes it!" Mara laughed, trying to push the puppy away.

"Dit — to!" Aaron called out, and quickly the puppy raced to the small boy, tugging at his sleeves. Iliana stood and watched, laughing, as the pup ran from one child to the other at the sound of the name.

"Okay, okay. Ditto is now your official name." Mara bent down close to the puppy as he licked her face, cleaning the area around her mouth.

"All right, supper is on the table. Get washed up and ready to eat!" Micah called out, turning away from the excitement to take the meatloaf out of the oven. Mara gave Ditto one last hug and rushed to the kitchen sink to wash her hands. Ditto tried to follow, but was scooped up by Ben and placed in the temporary barricade he had constructed with folding chairs around the new puppy impoundment area.

◆

Ben helped clear the table while Iliana and Mara rushed into the laundry room to play with the puppy. Aaron followed, stepping not too carefully into the area. "Yuck! It — stick — y!" moaned Aaron, looking at the bottom of his foot.

"Oh, sick! Mom! Come quick!" screamed Mara.

Micah walked over, smelling the situation immediately. "It's just puppy doo doo, nothing to worry about." She handed Aaron a paper towel, saying, "Just wipe it off of your foot. It won't kill you."

"But it smells so bad!" cried Mara. She huddled in the corner with Iliana and Ditto as Micah helped Aaron clean the mess from the bottom of his foot. Ditto jumped excitedly with all of the attention. "Can we do anything about it?"

"Well, puppy poop smells bad, and there isn't any thing that you can do about that. But you can train puppies to go to the bathroom outside, or else they do it wherever they happen to be," Micah explained.

"How do we train him? We need to do it quick, before someone else steps in it and stinks up the house," Mara pleaded, recovering slightly from the odor.

Walking over from the kitchen, Ben thought that he knew the answer. "You just take him outside for a walk, and they kind of know to go – it's just nature. Then pet him and say 'Good Boy!' And if he has an accident inside the house, just holler 'No!', or rub his nose in the poop, or bop him with a rolled up newspaper."

"No – bop – puppy!" said Aaron emphatically, now totally cleaned up and rolling on the ground with Ditto. "Dit – to – nice – pup – py."

"And no way are you going to rub his nose into the poop! He would be sick if he had to smell it that close!" Mara said.

Micah stood up, threw the paper towel in the trash, and turned to the children. "Well, you will just have to take turns taking him outside till he learns." She heard the rain beating down hard on the laundry room door and continued. "But not tonight – it's raining too hard. We'll start first thing in the morning with his training. Until then, just be careful not to step in anything, and we'll spread newspapers around to try to keep the area clean."

Micah heard the phone ringing and turned to answer it, leaving the laundry room full of laughing, playing children. She felt a drip on her head as she went to the kitchen to answer the phone, looking up to where the laundry room roof joined the main house roof to see a leak starting from the rain. "Five minutes, and then get ready for bed!" Micah hollered at the children before picking up the phone.

"Mrs. Summers?" a voice spoke from the telephone receiver.

"Yes, this is Micah Summers," Micah answered, trying to recognize the voice.

"I'm sorry to be calling you so late, but I was a little worried. This is Luke Johnson from over at the plant. We've been getting a lot of rain, and the weather radar looks like it might keep raining right through the night." Luke paused, listening for a response. He wasn't sure why he had felt the need to call Micah, after meeting her only briefly. He wasn't sure how his call would be received. She didn't respond during his pause, so he went on nervously. "The, uh, weather man says we might get up to ten inches of rain, and I was thinking about you living down there close to the Dry Coyote Creek."

"Dry Coyote Creek?" Somewhere in back of Micah's mind the words sounded familiar. She had remembered her grandparents saying the words, but never knew what they referred to. "You mean the dry creek behind our place?"

"Yeah, it usually doesn't carry any water, but when it rains really hard, it can overflow and do a little flooding. I don't know if it floods there at your home, but I just thought I would warn you to keep an eye out." Luke looked over at Amy Lynn playing quietly with a doll in her bed. She had come home talking about the two new girls in her class, and seemed very close to them. Luke wondered if he had called because of Amy Lynn, or if he was attracted to Micah. "Listen, I don't want to sound out of place or anything, but if you think you need any help at all, please don't hesitate to give me a call 661-1313. That's the number down at the plant, and it forwards to me at night if there is an emergency."

"Well, thank you very much, Mr. Johnson, this is very nice of you." Micah remembered his pleasant smile from earlier. "I'm sure we'll be all right, but I'll keep a close eye out. And if we get into any trouble, I will be sure to give you a call," Micah said as she quickly wrote Luke Johnson's name and number on a strawberry shaped note pad.

"Okay, then, good night Mrs. Summers, ya'll be careful."

"Goodnight, Mr. Johnson, and thank you again." Micah wondered as she saw that she had doodled happy faces all around Luke Johnson's name. She quickly put it out of her mind and turned back toward the children.

"All right! Ben, Mara, Aaron, Iliana, time to stop playing with the puppy and get ready for bed!" Micah thought about telling the children about what Luke Johnson had said about the possible flooding, but decided not to worry them. "I want baths for everyone, and straight to bed." She noticed as the children filed through that the dripping above the laundry room door had gotten worse.

"Aw, Mom! Can't we please stay up? There's no school tomorrow, so we can sleep in late in the morning," Mara pleaded, holding onto Iliana's hand.

Micah bent into the kitchen cabinet to grab a pot for the dripping water. "Sorry, Mara, but we might have a big day tomorrow," Micah said, thinking about cleaning up down at the creek. She wondered if the chicken pen might flood. "Straight to bed after your bath, and don't stay up too late talking to Iliana."

"All right, Mom. I love you! Are you coming up to say prayers?" Mara called out.

Micah carefully placed the pot under the dripping water, watching the four children scamper up the stairs, laughing and playing. "Sure thing, in just a minute. Let me clean up a little and I'll be right up."

Mara

Mara woke early, and stared into the darkness. She felt the comfort of Iliana sleeping beside her and snuggled against her. She always felt so safe and comfortable when Iliana was there. It was almost as if she could not remember being without her.

A strange whine drifted up from downstairs that startled Mara. She listened quietly, and then heard it again. "The puppy!" she thought, and listened more carefully. Again, the puppy whined, and Mara thought she could hear scratching on the door.

She quickly sat up and put on a long warm pullover that she had gotten for last year's birthday. She quietly eased out of bed, slipped on her shoes, tiptoed out the bedroom, and started down the stairs. The whining and scratching became louder as she approached the laundry room. She almost tripped over the pot that Micah had placed on the floor under the leak at the laundry room entrance, spilling some of the water from the full pot. "Ditto! What's the matter, Boy?" she whispered loudly.

Ditto immediately rushed to Mara, and jumped on her lap, licking her face. His tail was wagging nonstop. Mara hugged and petted the puppy, and together they lay on the floor for a few moments. "Good boy, Ditto! It's Okay; you don't need to be afraid. You're safe here!" Mara spoke softly to the puppy.

Ditto lay quietly for a few moments, and then went back to the door. He looked at Mara, and began softly whining. "What is it, boy? Do you want to go home?" Mara reached out again for the puppy, and suddenly remembered the events of the night before, and the awful smell of the puppy poop. Ditto began softly scratching at the door.

"That's it. Isn't it, Ditto. You need to go the bathroom!" Mara thought about what Ben has said about walking the dog outside, and the consequences of his going to the bathroom inside the home. "Nobody's going to rub your nose in poop!" Mara stood up and looked around for a string to use as a leash for Ditto, but found nothing. She decided to walk the puppy outside and just stay close to him. Remembering the rain from the day before, she put on a raincoat hanging close to the door and grabbed an umbrella. Mara opened the door carefully, holding Ditto by his brown leather collar. The rain had slowed, and was now only a slight drizzle. The sky was just beginning to lighten in the east where the sun was rising behind the still dark, but thinning clouds. Ditto jumped out of the door, but Mara kept a firm grip on the collar.

"Slow down, Ditto! Let's get away from the house a little before you have to go!" Mara and Ditto walked toward the back of the house toward the chicken pen. Mara could hear the mother hen clucking softly at her chicks, and an unfamiliar sound roaring in the distance. "This looks like a good spot! Over here by the tree! Come on Ditto. This can be your bathroom!" Mara walked Ditto to the small tree at the front of the chicken pen, and carefully let him go. Ditto slowly walked to the tree, sniffed several times and relieved himself. "Good boy, Ditto! Good boy!" Mara remembered Ben's words from the night before, and felt proud of her accomplishment. "Nobody's gonna rub your nose in poop. Good boy!"

Suddenly, a quail lifted from a nearby bush, and flew straight out behind the chicken coop. Ditto bolted, and ran after the low flying bird in the near darkness. "Ditto, No!" Mara commanded, and started to rush after the fleeing puppy.

◆

Waking suddenly, Iliana felt a rush of fear. "Mara" she cried out softly. She turned quickly and saw the empty side of the bed where Mara had slept. Sensing gathering panic, Iliana sat up quickly, and got out of bed. She glanced quickly around the room, and not seeing Mara anywhere, rushed out of the room toward the stairs, not bothering to put on her shoes or robe. Halfway down the stairs, Iliana saw the spilled pot of water near the laundry room entrance.

◆

Ditto rushed behind the chicken coop, all senses concentrating on the fleeing bird. Mara followed as closely as she could in the near darkness. Suddenly, Ditto stopped abruptly and began barking fiercely. Running toward him, Mara stumbled and fell, slipping in the mud, sliding down the slope feet first. She neared Ditto and reached out for him, then felt her feet slide into a wet, cold torrent.

◆

Iliana stopped abruptly, feeling a sense of cold gathering in her body. Tears in her eyes, she flung the laundry room door open and rushed out the back of the house toward the chicken pen.

◆

Mara felt the strong tug at her feet, grasping her unrelentingly. She struggled against the pull, but felt herself being dragged in deeper, and deeper. "Help!" she cried out against the roaring water, but the current and the noise carried her cry away. Ditto quickly sensed her struggle, and jumped into the rising current, barking loudly. He grasped at her outreached hand, and clasped onto her sleeve, straining furiously against the pull.

◆

"Mara!" Iliana screamed into the gathering morning and the drizzling rain. She tried to call out again, but felt the air being taken from her, her lungs unable to breathe. She felt cold and confused, completely disoriented by the overwhelming sensations. Rushing blindly toward the back of the chicken pen, she heard a frightened barking slowly disappear into the sound of the raging creek, drifting rapidly downstream. She dropped at the side of the creek, sobbing uncontrollably, overcome by stabbing cold and confusion, still feeling as though she couldn't breath. Slowly, she could no longer try to catch her breath and felt the cold and confusion completely overtake her. She collapsed on the side of the creek, sobbing, as the sound of the puppy disappeared completely into the morning.

◆

Aaron awoke and slowly looked around. He felt as though something was wrong. He saw Ben still sleeping, and went to the window. He saw the rain falling slowly against the window pane, and the eastern sky beginning to lighten. He looked down toward the chicken pen, and saw a strange dark shape filling the ravine behind the pens. He thought he could see movement through the ravine; trees, branches, but he was not sure what he was seeing. Near the ravine, he thought he could just make out a small, white figure.

"Ben, — wake — up!" Aaron spoke urgently, prodding his brother. "Some – thing – wrong!" Ben woke slowly and sat up in bed. He looked at his brother, and saw fear filling his face. "Ben, — wake — up! Need — help!"

"Okay, sure, Aaron. What's the matter! What going on?" Ben looked carefully at his brother, trying to discern the crisis.

"Need — help! Go — tell — Mom!' Aaron said, as he left Ben's side and headed out the door toward the hall leading to Micah's bedroom.

Ben slipped on his shoes and got out of bed hurriedly, following Aaron to Micah's door. He noticed that the door to Mara's room was open, and quickly glanced down the stairs. He saw the spilled water in the laundry room entrance, and remembered Ditto.

"Mom! Wake — up! Some – thing – bad – wrong." Ben entered his mom's room, and saw Aaron pulling on Micah.

Micah sat up halfway in bed, and lifted Aaron beside her. "What is it Aaron. You okay?" she asked, softly, hugging Aaron, trying to comfort him. She looked up to see Ben coming toward the bed. "Ben, is everything all right?"

"I don't know, Mom, Aaron just woke me up, saying something is wrong," Ben said sleepily.

"What's wrong, Aaron? Tell Mom. It'll be okay," Micah tried to soothe Aaron's fears.

Ben remembered Mara's open door and the spilled water at the bottom of the stairs. "Mom, I'm going to go and check on the puppy.

Maybe Aaron thinks that there is something wrong down there." Ben left the side of Micah's bed and headed toward the stairs, listening as Micah continued to comfort Aaron.

When Ben reached the bottom of the steps and entered the laundry room, he immediately noticed the back door was open, and that the drizzling rain was entering into the laundry room. Glancing quickly around, he saw that the puppy was gone.

"Mom, the back door is open, and I think that the puppy might have gone outside!" Ben hollered up the steps to his mom. "It's not raining too hard. I'm gonna go outside to look for Ditto." Ben slipped into his boots by the rear door and stepped out into the drizzling rain, closing the door behind him.

◆

"Mom! Something – bad – wrong!" Aaron continued, pleading with his mom to get out of bed.

'What is it, Aaron? What's wrong?" Micah watched Aaron carefully, trying to understand his anxiety. Her concern mounted looking at Aaron's face.

"Angel – hurt! On – ground – by – chickens!" Aaron cried.

Micah stared silently at Aaron, trying to comprehend what he was trying to communicate. His eyes were pleading, searching Micah's face. He pulled on her hand, trying to pull her out of the bed.

"Okay, hold on just a second." Micah tried to calm Aaron, stepping out of bed and into her shoes and grabbing her robe. "Let's go see what's wrong."

Aaron led his mother down the hall toward the stairs. Micah slowed when she passed Mara's room and saw the door open. "Mara? Iliana?" Micah stopped at the door, pulling Aaron into the room. She quickly looked around and saw that the children were gone. A sense of dread began to fill Micah, and she began to hurry out of the room. She quickly picked Aaron up and put him on her hip, heading toward the stairs.

"Angel — hurt! Mom — help!" Aaron looked down the stairs and quickly back up at Micah.

"Aaron, calm down. Everything is okay." Micah tried to reassure Aaron, but the increasing anxiety showed in her voice. She reached the bottom of the steps, and walked quickly into the laundry room. She opened the back door, and called out "Ben! Ben! Where are you?" Staring out into the early morning drizzle, she grabbed an umbrella.

◆

Ben reached the chicken coop quickly, stepping over the puddles as best he could. "Ditto! Ditto! Here boy! Come here, boy!" He continued walking, searching through the slowly falling rain. Ben quickly glanced in the coop, seeing the hen setting high out of the rain. He glanced back behind the pen and saw the swollen creek passing through the usually dry ravine. Large tree branches and boxes drifted quickly, entangling on a refrigerator that had become lodged against a large tree. As he slowly took in the scene in front of him, he spotted a small, white figure lying beside the water. "Mara!" he yelled, as he rushed toward the edge of the water.

He reached the figure and reached to pull her over, and saw the pale face of the small, wet child in front of him. It wasn't Mara. "Iliana!" he called out, turning her over carefully so that he could view her face. The sound of the roaring current was deafening, absorbing his words as they came out of his mouth. Iliana was motionless, and her face stained with mud and grass. Ben brushed the wet hair from her face, and looked at her closed eyes. "Wake up, Iliana! Wake up!" He wasn't sure if he could see her breathing or not. Panic quickly filled him as he sat by the water. "Mom! Mom! Come quick! Behind the chicken coop!" Ben hollered into the morning rain, hoping that his mom could hear him, not able to decide whether to leave Iliana to get help or to stay by her side. He frantically looked up and down the swollen gorge for signs of Mara and Ditto.

◆

Micah heard Ben's call, and grasping Aaron tightly to her side, said a quiet prayer as she ran toward the chicken pens. "Ben! I'm coming!" she called out. She stumbled over a fallen branch, and headed toward her eldest son's panicked cries. Fear began to envelope her as she viewed the swollen ravine behind the pens. Rain began to mix with tears as she struggled to get to the fallen figures beside the raging water. "O Lord, please. O Lord, help us," Micah prayed quietly into the rain.

◆

Iliana's eyes slowly opened as she heard a familiar cry in the distance. She saw Ben holding her, with fear in his eyes. She heard the quiet prayers of Micah, and the rush of the raging waters. Suddenly, she remembered – remembered the last feelings before she had passed out. She closed her eyes tightly against the memory, trying to make it go away, to change. Tears began to stream from her face.

"Iliana! Wake up!" Ben called, seeing the young girl's eyes briefly open. "Mom, come here!"

Micah quickly got to Ben cradling the small white figure. Firmly holding onto Aaron's hand, she sat him on the ground and knelt beside Ben, gently pushing him out of the way. She placed her hand behind Iliana's head and lifted it, calling out her name.

Iliana's eyes opened, and she gazed at Micah. She saw the fear in Micah's eyes, and felt it reflected in her own heart. Micah's eyes broke away briefly, searching desperately up and down the raging torrent of water. Her eyes quickly returned to Iliana's, and Iliana watched as Micah tried to force a smile. "Iliana, are you okay?"

Iliana knew the real question that Micah had in her heart, and tried to answer. "Mara." Iliana heard the name come from her own mouth, but could say no more. Tears clouded her eyes. She struggled to shut them from the world.

"Iliana, honey, please stay awake!" Micah heard desperation in her own voice. "Iliana. Mara! Where is Mara?"

Iliana opened her eyes briefly, and again saw Micah's pain and fear. She could not answer.

Micah felt Iliana trembling beneath her hands, and looked quickly at Ben and Aaron. The roar of the water made it difficult to think, and the drizzle had again turned into a steady light rain, washing Micah's hair into her eyes. She felt herself tremble in the cold, and reached out to Aaron, pulling him in toward her.

"Mara!" Micah heard her own voice rise against the rain and creek. "Mara!" Looking up and down the banks of the water, she fought panic and tried to clear her thoughts. "Ben, go into the house and look for Mara. Look everywhere, and come back quickly."

She could hear Aaron crying out, quietly, "Mara. Mara — where — are — you?" She looked down again at Iliana, and saw the young girl with eyes tightly closed, soaking in the rain. Instinctively, she gently picked up Iliana and tucked the young girl on her shoulder while holding Aaron's hand tightly. She followed Ben back to the house. "Mara, — Mara — where — are — you?" she heard Aaron crying into the rain as she quickly made her way.

◆

Micah laid Iliana carefully on the couch. "Aaron, please go to the bathroom and get a towel. Quickly!" She brushed the damp hair out of Iliana's face and softly called to her again. "Iliana, Iliana!" She watched as Iliana kept her eyes closed, saying nothing.

"Ben, did you see Mara?" Micah heard Ben coming down the stairs.

"Mom, I can't find her anywhere! She must be outside!" Ben's voice became louder as he continued down the stairs, and Micah sensed her young son's rising panic. "I'm going to go outside and look!"

"Mara — not — in — bathroom." Aaron returned to Micah's side, carefully handing her the towel.

Micah gently dried Iliana's face. "Ben, come here." Micah's thoughts raced as she tried to fight her growing terror. She looked out the window, and saw the falling rain, remembering again the swollen creek. She did not want Ben near the water.

'Dry Coyote Creek' — she remembered Luke Johnson's voice — and his warning.

"Ben, look on the table! I wrote a name and phone number on a pad."

Ben found the strawberry shaped pad. There, written among doodled smiling happy faces was a name and number. "Mom, I think I found it! Luke Johnson?"

"Yes, that's it!" Micah remembered small bits of the conversation from the night before. "Mr. Johnson called last night, and offered help if we needed it. Ben, listen carefully! Call Mr. Johnson, and tell him that we have trouble." Micah thought carefully about what to tell Ben, not wanting to frighten him. "Tell him that we are looking for Mara, that she might be outside somewhere." Micah stopped briefly, fighting the tears in her eyes, and trying to calm the trembling she heard in her voice. "Ask him to come quickly, and to call the sheriff."

Micah reached instinctively to Aaron and wrapped her arms around him. She felt him shivering from the cold. Looking at Iliana's still body, she felt herself quietly crying. "Aaron, stay here. Stay here beside Iliana and keep her inside." She quickly got up and pulled a blanket from the hall closet, wrapping it over Iliana and around Aaron. "I'm going to go outside and find Mara. Promise me, I need you to stay inside."

"Stay – inside – with – angel." Aaron said quietly, snuggling against Iliana trying to stay warm.

"Yes, Aaron, just stay inside. Everything is going to be all right." Micah tried to reassure herself, as well as Aaron. She rose and turned toward the back door.

"Mom, I got ahold of Mr. Johnson! He said that he would come right over, and that he would call the sheriff, too!" Ben met Micah at the back door, and began to pull on his own boots. Micah looked at Ben, and realized how much she had grown to depend on him. She considered allowing him to go with her to look for Mara, but knew that it would be too hazardous.

"Ben, listen carefully!" Micah began as she started to step out into the rain. "I'm going to go back where we found Iliana and look for Mara. She's got to be out there somewhere. I need you to stay here at the house and make sure that Aaron and Iliana are all right, and to keep an eye out for Mr. Johnson and the sheriff." Micah started walking away from the house toward the raging water. She turned back toward Ben, trying to hide the fearful tears in her eyes. "Ben, I love you! Everything is going to be all right! Just stay inside and wait for help!" Micah tore her eyes away from Ben and headed toward the sounds of the water. She stumbled again near the chicken pen on the fallen branch, and picked herself back up. Tears streamed from her face as she began calling into the morning. "Mara! Mara! Where are you? Mara!"

Torment

The sheriff turned down the long driveway, feeling his rear tires slipping in the thick mud that had been nothing but dust the day before. He felt the front tires slip into the deep tracks of the truck that he followed from town, having watched it turn hurriedly from the uranium mine entrance. The sheriff had barely made it across the low water crossing where Dry Coyote Creek crossed the road from town, and couldn't remember seeing that much water in these parts. Almost two feet deep, and over two hundred feet wide where it crossed the road, the creek was an ugly, angry brown mixture of water, mud, and debris that it had picked up from the countryside. Even though the rain had let up overnight, it was still falling, letting little light into the gathering morning. He pulled on the steering wheel, urging his tires out of the rut, and reached for his coffee cup. It had been a long night, and he had stayed up most of it listening to weather reports and putting up barriers at low water crossings. It seemed that Hondo was catching the worst of the storm as it stalled over the central Texas area. Hopefully the storm would move on before someone got hurt, he thought. He felt his front wheel slide back down into the rut, spilling his coffee on his still damp rain poncho. "Damn," the sheriff heard himself say quietly, wondering what kind of problems were at the Summers' place.

Braking to a stop, the sheriff saw the oldest Summers boy rush out to the truck in front him. Luke Johnson quickly opened his door, and slid on a bright yellow rain poncho with the uranium plant symbol spread across the back. As the sheriff opened his own patrol car door, he wondered how Luke had become involved in the Summers' affairs. He saw the Summers boy point excitedly behind the house, and then saw Luke point quickly toward the sheriff before heading down toward the creek. The sheriff could see the brown, murky water from the driveway, speeding up as it narrowed behind the Summers' chicken pens.

"Sheriff, Sheriff! Mara's gone!" Ben spilled out, rushing toward the sheriff in the mud and rain. The sheriff saw him almost slip in the mud as he approached him.

"Hold on, Boy! Slow down and tell me what's going on!" The sheriff balanced himself against the front of his patrol car, reaching down to adjust his two way radio, trying to keep it dry. He looked up again behind Ben and saw Micah and Luke rushing toward each other. He could hear their rising voices against the rain, but he couldn't make out what they were saying.

"Mom's back behind the house looking for Mara. When I got up this morning, she was gone. I think she might have gone outside with a puppy we found last night! We can't find her!" Ben blurted out. "I found Iliana down by the river, but she's unconscious, or something, cause she's not saying anything! Mom told me to stay inside the house and take care of everything till you got here. I could hear her down behind the chicken pens, calling out to Mara. I looked everywhere in the house, and couldn't find her!"

Ben was out of breath by the time he got to the last information. The Sheriff was listening to him as he looked out over Ben's head, trying to sort out the information. He saw Luke take off his rain poncho and place it over Micah, and start off down the river, cupping his hands to his mouth. Micah slumped over, her hands on her face. The sheriff's gaze fell onto the house, where he could see small hands wiping away the condensation from the large window in the front room of the house, and could see Aaron's face pushing against the glass, looking out at the sheriff and Ben. His eyes fell back to Ben just as he was finishing. He looked into Ben's eyes, and recognized excitement, confusion and fear. The sheriff grabbed hold of the front of his car, and carefully lowered himself to one knee, trying to get close to the boy, and hear him carefully, now giving him full attention.

"Tell me again. Who's missing?" The sheriff listened intently as Ben repeated his story, almost starting over from the beginning. The sheriff sorted out that the boy thought that his sister was missing. "Did you look everywhere in the house? Are you sure she's not inside?" The sheriff listened as Ben listed all of the rooms that he had searched while waiting. Again he looked out over the boy's head to the creek. He could no longer see Luke, but Micah had turned toward the house and was approaching him. He carefully pulled himself up from the boy, and walked toward Micah.

"Mrs. Summers, everything all right?" The sheriff asked, knowing that things were bad, but still trying to get a handle on the scope of the problem. He could see a mixture of mud and tears streaming down Micah's face.

"Sheriff, please, help me! It's my little girl, Mara! I can't find her anywhere!" The sheriff heard the panic in Micah's voice, and struggled to remain calm and professional against his own rising fears. He looked again toward the creek, and saw no sign of Luke. He could see Micah trembling from fear and cold.

"Come on, Mrs. Summers, let's get you and the boy here inside and out of the rain and talk about this." The sheriff placed his heavy arm carefully around Micah and led her toward the back door while placing one hand on Ben's shoulder. Walking toward the door, he heard the rising roar of the creek, and thought he could make out the sound of Luke calling out a name. He could feel Micah trembling under his arm.

The sheriff opened the rear door and wiped his boots on the rear mat. He saw the spilled pot near the doorway, and noticed the rapid drip of the rain from the ceiling. He watched as Aaron came running to his mom, almost slipping in the growing spill of water.

"Mom — Angel — dying!" Aaron reached out for Micah's hand, and began to furiously pull her toward the living room and the couch.

Micah tried to compose herself as she reached out her hand to wipe her face and she followed Aaron, saying nothing. The sheriff followed Ben into the living room.

Iliana lay on the couch, almost lifeless. She was covered with a damp towel, and wrapped carefully with a blanket, neatly tucked in all around her. Aaron bent closely toward her, pulling his mother closer. "See? — Angel — not — awake!"

Micah bent down to Iliana, and dried her own hand on the towel before reaching out to Iliana. She carefully brushed the hair from Iliana's forehead, and called her name quietly. "Iliana," Micah began, "Iliana, wake up." The sheriff saw the young girl's eyes slowly open and gaze at Micah. The gaze seemed intent, but brief. Tears quickly filled the young girl's eyes, and the sheriff saw her shut them tightly, turning her head away from Micah.

"Mom! Angel — won't — wake — up! Angel — dying!" Aaron stood attentively beside where Micah was bent over Iliana.

The sheriff reached out and instinctively patted Ben on the shoulder. He bent down toward the young girl on the couch. " 'Liana? I need you to wake up! This is the sheriff, and I need to talk to you!" The sheriff looked at Iliana intently, watching for signs of distress. Her breathing was slow, but normal. He could feel her slow pulse as he gently wrapped his giant fingers around her wrist. Her skin felt cool, almost cold, but she was not shivering. He could see her eyes closed tightly, almost forced shut, as if fighting back from opening. A sliver of a tear formed at the corner of her eye. He slowly raised himself from her side, and turned to Micah.

"Mrs. Summers? I think she's all right." The sheriff watched Micah as her eyes turned toward his. He could see that her eyes were bloodshot from crying. "Do you think that you could tell me what's going on?"

The sheriff listened as Micah related the same information that Ben had given earlier, adding that she had gone to the creek to search for Mara. Micah had tried to compose herself as she told about going up and down the water's edge, calling out Mara's name, how she had not seen any sign of her six year old daughter. "Sheriff, please help us! We have to find her! She must be cold out in the rain!"

The sheriff reached for his radio and began to turn away from Micah. He sensed the urgency of the situation, and his years of experience began to kick in, detaching himself from the fears and panic of the Summers family, protecting his rational senses from the building emotions within himself. He felt the resolve within himself building, and turned on the radio.

"Dispatch, come in!" the sheriff commanded into the radio. He began to walk to the rear door, slowly, trying to sort out what had happened.

"Dispatch, Sheriff. We're here. Come in." the sheriff heard the radio respond to his request, and he began to formulate a plan.

"We have a missing child out here at the Summers residence on the county road. We are going to need a search team as soon as possible."

The sheriff quickly thought of all possible outcomes, and solutions. "You might want to call Kimble County, and see if they can put their water rescue team on notice. We might need their help out here in this water."

The sheriff listened to his radio as the dispatch confirmed his information, and began to call for additional help. He turned toward the living room and saw Micah, holding Ben and Aaron closely, sobbing quietly. He tried to formulate something comforting to say, but the insulation from his own emotions would not let him. "Mrs. Summers, I suggest you and the children stay inside. I got help on the way, and we are going to do everything we can to find that little girl of yours." The sheriff wasn't sure if Micah was listening. "Why don't you and the boys check the house one more time, and look for any clues as to where she might have gone off to," the sheriff suggested, trying to think of something that might distract them from their own feelings. The sheriff opened the back door, and slowly but determinedly, walked out into the rain. He pulled his rain poncho up over his head and tight up around his shoulders. He saw Luke Johnson coming back from downstream, his hands cupped around his mouth as he called out. The sheriff began to walk quickly toward Luke. "Damn!"

◆

The sheriff took off the rain poncho and laid it on the top of the car, hoping that it would dry off before he stored it in the trunk. He opened the front door of his car and reached for a towel, drying his thinning hair and forehead. He reached for his hat and placed in on his head, pulling it down tight against the breeze. The rain had finally let up, but the sheriff felt his damp clothes sticking against his body. He saw his empty coffee thermos, and felt the weight of a long day against him. Dark was closing in, but the sheriff was hoping that the day would not yet end.

Walking toward him, his deputy announced, "Sheriff, we've searched the high end of the property again, and haven't seen any signs." The sheriff leaned against his car heavily, and looked up at his deputy. He looked toward the creek at the truck and trailer parked nearby. He had not heard from the water rescue team from Kimble County for over an hour, and wondered how long they might stay into the night. He knew that it would not be long.

"Where do you want us to search now?" The sheriff looked into his deputy's face, and saw long lines under his eyes beneath the mud. He knew that his deputy had been up most of the night too, and must be growing weary. Overhead, he could hear the sounds of a helicopter coming closer.

"I don't know, Dan." The sheriff looked up toward the house, and squinted his eyes to see into the windows. He did not want to go back into the house, not now, not with night coming. He didn't want to talk to Mrs. Summers again, not without knowing something more. "Let's go talk to the chopper boys and see if they found anything."

"You want a sandwich, or something to drink?" The pastor's voice was cheerful, full of eternal hope, offering comfort from the back of his aging sedan. He and his wife had been present for almost the entire afternoon, offering food and drink, comforting the Summers family whenever they could.

"No, thank you, not right now." The sheriff tried to force returning a smile, but wasn't able to. He turned to see the helicopter landing in the clearing near the hackberry tree. Pulling his hat down tightly against the wind from the turning blades, he quickly walked toward them. He watched as the pilot climbed down and started to walk toward the sheriff.

"Sheriff, we haven't seen a sign of that little girl!" The pilot's voice was raised, hollering over the sound of his whirling blades. "We thought we might have seen a little white dog down the creek about a mile and a half. We tried to put down near the spot, but couldn't find anywhere to land." The pilot looked down to the ground, shaking his head.

The sheriff could sense frustration and disappointment in his manner. "Maybe we didn't see anything. It could have just been some trash blowing in the wind," the pilot continued looking up at the sheriff. The pilot looked back toward the creek, and up towards the sky. Patches of blue were beginning to show near where the sun was setting, a sign of hope for clear weather the next day.

The sheriff knew that it was getting late, and the pilot was waiting for permission to leave before dark. The sheriff looked down the creek, and saw a group of men with ropes and lifejackets heading toward the pastor's sedan.

"You seen any sign of Luke Johnson and his boys?" The sheriff asked, turning back toward the pilot. Luke Johnson and a group of men from the uranium mine had headed down the creek, and had not been heard from in several hours, having lost radio contact. Luke had told the sheriff that he would stay out all night if he had to, that he was not going to give up on the lost child.

"Yeah, Sheriff, we stopped and talked to them before we started heading back. They hadn't seen anything, either. They had plenty of gear, and said that they were going to stay out looking until they found her…" The pilot's voice trailed off, looking back toward the creek. The pilot and sheriff shared a knowledge that neither one would admit to, knowing what the likely outcome was going to be with dark fast approaching. "We did tell them about where we thought we saw the dog, and they might be making their way back upstream to get there."

The sheriff reached down and grabbed his belt, pulling up on his wet pants. He looked again toward the water rescue team, and saw them accepting the offered sandwiches and drinks. He knew that they had not found anything. "Okay, let's call it a day. You boys be careful flying out!" The sheriff nodded his head toward the pilot, and heard the sound of the helicopter blades increasing after the pilot gave the thumbs up to his waiting copilot.

The pilot turned briefly back to the sheriff. "We'll be ready to go at daylight, if you still need us!" the pilot shouted, turning and jogging to the helicopter and climbing back into his seat.

The sheriff and his deputy talked briefly with the water rescue crew, and made arrangements for them to come out the next morning. No one had seen anything, other than small dog prints along the shore in several areas. The rescue team tried to sound optimistic, but the sheriff knew that they were losing hope. "Thank you, boys. You did a great job!" The sheriff wanted to return their hopefulness with gratitude. "Unless you hear different, I'll see you here at daybreak." The sheriff left his deputy with the rescue crew, who were accepting another round of sandwiches. He tried to say something to the pastor and his wife, but no words came out. He felt a tear begin to break into his eye, and he turned away from their smiling faces. He wiped his face, and turned toward the Summers' house.

The sheriff reached Micah's front door quickly, too quickly. He had not had time to formulate words that might give hope and encouragement. He watched as Micah stood up from the couch and approached, leaving Iliana covered with a blanket. Ben and Aaron trailed beside her. As she opened the door, the sheriff began, "I'm sorry..." and then his voice trailed off.

Goodbye

"Over here!" The sound of the barking puppy had drawn the attention of the group. Luke Johnson fought his way through the weeds and scrub brush to the front of his men. He was muddy and exhausted. He and his men had found little comfort or sleep during the night, pausing for only a few hours, laying on a tarp that they had brought to protect themselves from the soaking ground. His feet were sloshing inside of his damp socks inside of his rubber boots, ankles swollen with blisters from the stings of the fire ants. The men had fought their way back up the creek to the location near where the chopper pilot had directed them, but had to stop searching until morning. The early morning sunrise had brought out hope for the day, along with a steamy, humid morning.

Luke spied the dog first, barking excitedly at his crew chief. Muddy, but with two large identical black spots on either side of his white back, the puppy did not move from his location, and seemed agitated, determined to hold his ground. "Ditto?" Luke searched his memory for the name of the puppy that was missing, along with Mara. Ben had told him all about finding the puppy, how they had kept it over night, and that it was missing along with Mara. "Ditto, here boy!" The puppy wagged his tail upon hearing the name, but continued to bark. It was when Luke was reaching out to calm the puppy that he saw the outstretched hand in the branches. The hand was small and pale, and had a grip on a limb. From behind the hand he followed the arm and could just make out a small face, eyes closed, brown hair matted with mud. Except for her face, the small child's body was completely submerged.

"Mara?" Luke called out, almost quietly, and he moved quickly toward her. As he reached out to touch her arm, the puppy raced toward his hand, grabbing his sleeve and trying to pull him from the young girl.

"Ditto, it's okay," Luke said, just above a whisper. The other men caught up to Luke quickly and stopped suddenly behind him, not saying a word. They watched as Luke reached again for the small arm, grasping it firmly in his hand.

◆

"Mara!" Iliana sat up suddenly from Micah's bed, startling Micah. All night she had become more and more quiet, hardly moving at all. The sheriff had called a doctor to take a look at her early in the previous afternoon, and he had found everything physically normal. But Micah knew that something was seriously wrong. It had seemed as if the glow that Iliana had since she had first seen her had somehow faded, was somehow less visible. She hadn't said a word all day, and would not open her eyes or even lift her head from the couch. Micah had put her quietly into her own bed for the night so that she could keep a close watch on her.

Ben and Aaron were snuggled close to their mother's bed in the small floor area, wrapped in sleeping bags. They had not wanted to sleep in their own rooms. Aaron sat up, staring at Iliana. "Angel – talk!" Aaron said, pointing at Iliana. Micah sat up groggily, trying to think clearly. She had been unable to sleep through most of the night, even though she had taken the sleeping pills that the doctor had left her. She felt as though she had just fallen into a deep, long sleep.

"Mara!" Again Iliana cried out.

A flood of memories raced into Micah's mind, bringing the terror of the previous day into sharp focus. She looked at Iliana and saw her eyes wide open. She looked toward the door and searched the room desperately, hoping to see what Iliana was seeing. Seeing nothing, she turned back to Iliana. "Iliana, what honey, what is it?" Micah stared intently into Iliana's eyes, and felt Aaron climb up into her own lap.

"Mom! – Angel – talking! – Angel – not – dying!" Aaron snuggled close to Micah, pulling her blanket up over him while staring at Iliana.

Dying – Micah did not want to hear, or think, the word. She pulled Aaron close with one arm, and reached out to brush the hair from Iliana's face, asking her again "What is it, Iliana, what do you see?"

"Mara! I see Mara, by the water! Someone's holding her, carrying her! She's..." Iliana stared toward the door, and then suddenly turned towards Micah. "Mara's Mom, we must go quickly. Help me!" Iliana looked at Micah with pleading eyes briefly, and then watched as Micah threw back her covers and started to get out of bed. Micah stared in disbelief, not knowing what was happening.

Ben awoke from the noise and sat up. "Mom, what's going on? Did someone say they found Mara?" Ben watched as Iliana reached down for her shoes.

"Angel — not — dying! Angel — talking! — Angel — not — dying!" Aaron jumped out of Micah's lap and hurried to put on his own shoes. Iliana took Aaron's hand and started out the door. Aaron turned back to Micah and Ben. "Mom, — Ben — come — on! Angel — see — Mara!"

◆

"What the..." the sheriff muttered as he pulled down the driveway toward the Summers' home. He reached out in the early morning light to the center console in his patrol car to put down his coffee mug. In front of him, the sun was just beginning to rise out of a misty fog lifting from the receding waters in the creek. He slowed his car, watching the sight in front of him. He saw Iliana, walking, almost appearing to float in the fog. She was holding Aaron's hand. Close behind her followed Micah in her night clothes and slippers, holding onto Ben's hand. The four of them were heading from the house toward the chicken pen.

The sheriff pulled his car to a stop and opened the door. He lifted himself from the car, and stepped out onto the grass covered with heavy dew. "Mrs. Summers? Everything all right?" The sheriff was puzzled, not knowing what to say.

Micah turned toward the sheriff, still walking slowly and holding Ben's hand and tried to answer. "Sheriff, I don't know — it's Iliana. She woke up and said that she sees Mara. We're following where she goes." Micah looked confused and excited at the same time, the kind of excitement that hope brings to the hopeless.

The sheriff heard the buzz of the helicopter behind him as it approached. He looked up to see the pilot wave to him, heading out to check on Luke Johnson and his search party. The sheriff had talked to the pilot briefly before he left home. They had decided that, after checking on the search party, that they would begin to search the creek bed again in the daylight, continuing down the creek. But now, with the strange sight in front of him, the sheriff did not know what to do. He waved back at the pilot and began walking toward Micah.

"Wait up, Mrs. Summers. I'm going with you!" The sheriff hurried as fast as he could to catch up with Micah and the children as they rounded the back of the chicken coup.

◆

Luke gently lifted Mara's limp body from the water and placed her on ground. He took off his jacket and placed it over her. The other men from the search party gathered behind him, saying nothing. Ditto had stopped barking, and came close to Mara's face. As Ditto began to lick her face, Luke thought that he saw movement from Mara's mouth. He bent over close to her, and brushed the matted hair from her face.

"I think she's breathing!" Luke cried out, and quickly began to check Mara for signs of life. He thought that he might have felt a slow, slight pulse, but her skin was cold and damp. "I need something more to keep her warm. Give me your coat!" One of the rescuers quickly took off his jacket and wrapped it around the child. The sound of a helicopter could be heard approaching from the west, causing one of the men to stand and begin to wave his arms. Luke tilted Mara's head back carefully, trying to give her CPR, hoping to breathe life back into the child. "Please, Lord, let her live" Luke whispered in between slow, even breaths into the small girl.

The men searched the area frantically for a clearing for the helicopter, but the thick brush prevented any opportunity for landing. The pilot circled and spotted an open area about three quarters of a mile up the creek on high ground, about half way back to the Summers home. Circling back to the rescue party, the copilot wrote careful directions to the clearing on a note pad, wrapped the note around a small wrench and dropped it to the rescue party. He watched momentarily as the search party retrieved the note and gave the pilot a sign's up. As Luke and his men began to make preparations to move Mara to the clearing, the pilot turned back to the Summers' home and reached for the radio phone.

◆

"Well, could you see if she was alive, or moving?" The sheriff had turned his back away from Micah and the children, who were still following Iliana down the creek to the east. The trail along the creek was covered with debris from the flooding, but was grass covered and easy to walk on. The sheriff could hear the pilot's message clearly, but was not certain if he wanted Micah to hear any unconfirmed reports.

The pilot repeated that all he had seen was Luke trying to administer CPR, and was not even certain if the body was that of the missing child. He could only confirm that the search crew had appeared to be in contact with what seemed to be small child and that they were heading for the clearing.

"Well, head on to the clearing and get ready for air life transport to County General. I'll try to meet you there and give any help that I can!" The sheriff turned back toward Micah, and saw her pleading eyes looking at him, begging for information. He struggled with what he should tell her, but decided to tell her all that he knew.

"Micah, Luke Johnson and his boys may have found Mara a ways down the creek." The sheriff paused as he surveyed Micah's face, giving her a chance to brace herself for the information. "The helicopter pilot's not even sure if it is Mara, but they do have someone and they are making their way to a clearing to meet the pilot." Micah stood in front of the sheriff; silent, breathless, waiting. The sheriff felt a tear start to come to his own eye, and turned briefly away from Micah, looking up at the morning sky for just a brief moment. He looked down at the ground, composing himself, separating himself from all emotion. "Micah, the pilot doesn't know if who they found, if it is Mara, if she's even alive or not."

Micah suddenly stepped away from sheriff, looking down and shaking her head. She looked back at the sheriff with fierce, determined eyes. "Sheriff, we have to go! We have to go to where they are bringing her. Now!" Micah quickly turned around and began walking with determined steps toward the creek, in the direction that the children were already heading. She quickly caught up to Ben, Iliana, and Aaron, who were slowly making their way along the trail.

Micah picked up Aaron without a pause, and placed him on her hip. She took Ben's hand, and then suddenly stopped, turning back to the sheriff. "Sheriff, I need your help!"

The sheriff viewed the four persons in front of him. Micah stood defiantly, fighting tears, with one arm wrapped around a two year old holding on to her hip. She gripped the hand of her nine year old son in her other hand. Iliana stood beside Micah, stopping momentarily to look at the sheriff. Iliana appeared frail and weak, but alert and determined. The sheriff looked down at the ground and shook his head. He knew that he should demand that Micah return to the home with the children, that it was not safe for her to be out near the creek after the flooding from the day before, especially with the young children and Iliana having not fully recovered. He weighed the risks quickly, but knew at once that no matter what, he would probably not be able to convince Micah to stop. He knew that if he were in her shoes that he would continue.

"All right, then. Let's go." The sheriff walked quickly to Iliana, and picking her up carefully, started down the trail. She seemed light, as though she weighed almost nothing, and seemed very fragile. The sheriff wondered again if he was doing the right thing, and worried that someone might get hurt.

"Mara! We must go quickly!" The sheriff looked up from the trail into Iliana's face. The voice sounded quiet, almost flute like. Iliana stared straight at the sheriff for a few seconds, and then turned her gaze forward, as though she could see something that the sheriff could not.

The sheriff glanced back behind him to see Ben scampering, trying to keep up with the sheriff's long steps, and Micah close behind, carrying Aaron. He thought that he could hear Aaron singing, a familiar song that was just out of reach of the sheriff. The sheriff picked up his pace, and wiping away another tear from his own eye, moved toward the clearing, following the sound of the helicopter.

Resurrection

The blades of the helicopter had slowed, but the sound was still loud enough to make hearing difficult. Even though the helicopter had landed on the edge of the clearing some one hundred feet away, the slow turning blades still moved leaves and grass from the ground into a whirling motion near the trail.

The sheriff was winded and out of breath. He had wanted to stop several times. As light as Iliana was, carrying the child was exhausting for him. The trip had been made in silence except for the occasional wisps of the song from Aaron that he heard as they had walked. The helicopter pilot was the first person the sheriff saw as he approached the clearing. The pilot was running toward the opposite end of the clearing from where the sheriff was, hurrying toward an opening in the heavy brush. Just out of full sight in the opening, the sheriff thought he could make out several men in bright yellow jackets, with the man in front carrying something, or someone, wrapped in a yellow jacket.

"Mara!" The sheriff turned to Iliana, startled by the name spoken by the young girl. Stopping, the sheriff felt Iliana pulling from him, pushing him away. "Set me down! Now!" The sheriff bent over and carefully lowered Iliana to where her feet could touch the ground. He bent over to catch his breath, and as he did, he looked up to watch Iliana sprint forward to the opposite side of the clearing. Straightening back up slowly, he watched as first Ben, and then Micah, still carrying Aaron, ran past him.

Luke Johnson carried Mara into the clearing and dropped to one knee, holding her gently. He laid her carefully on the ground, just as Iliana, Micah, Ben, and Aaron reached the spot. His men quietly gathered around him, standing next to the helicopter pilot. The sheriff saw Luke look up toward him, and slowly shake his head before turning his gaze back to the young girl.

Micah set Aaron down, and knelt down beside Mara. She reached out her hand to Mara's face and touched her eyes, and then her mouth lovingly.

"I'm sorry. We were too late." Luke spoke slowly, carefully, fighting back his own tears. Micah reached down to Mara and pulled her up to her, holding her tightly, burying her own face into Mara's chest.

Luke looked up, and spoke to the sheriff. "I thought that we might have made it — it seemed like she was still alive when we found her." Luke bit deep into his lip to keep his composure. The sheriff heard a low, moaning sound coming from deep within Micah. Luke put his hand out to Micah, stroking her hair gently, and then slowly stood up. He walked to Ben and Aaron and wrapped them both in his arms and held them tight.

"Mara – dead?" Aaron spoke quietly, watching his mother and his sister next to him on the ground.

Luke looked up to see the sheriff gently take Iliana by the hand. "Yes, Aaron, Mara died. I'm sorry." Luke could feel Ben buried underneath his arm beginning to tremble with tears.

"Nobody – broke – Mara. She – just – die," Aaron looked up at Luke, and wiped a tear from Luke's face. "It – o – kay. Some – times – nothing – we – can – do."

Iliana let go of the sheriff's hand and walked slowly toward Micah and Mara, passing quietly by Luke, Ben, and Aaron. She touched Micah on the back of her hair, and bent down to where Mara was.

"Mara's Mom, don't cry." Iliana spoke quietly, confidently.

Micah felt a surge of peace spread from where Iliana had touched her. She lifted her head from Mara and looked at Iliana.

"Mara's Mom, don't cry," Iliana spoke again, now wiping the tears from Micah's face. Iliana smiled at Micah, and then looked down toward Mara. "I will take Mara to a better place, to a place where our Father is, to live forever."

"Mara," Iliana spoke directly to the young girl in her mother's arms. "Mara, come with me." Iliana reached toward Mara and took hold of both of her hands. Micah knelt up straight, releasing Mara into the hands of Iliana.

She watched, as slowly at first, and then faster and faster, the two figures seemed to spin around silently. Eyes closed, arms stretched out, fingers pointing to the end of time, they danced in the morning grass. The rising sun warmed their skin, and a soft wind blew their hair first into their faces and then behind them as they turned around and around.

Their tiptoes rose above the ground, whirling in a timeless motion as they floated effortlessly above a mist of endless joy.

Ben pulled loose from Luke and looked skyward. He looked through the morning mist, and saw wings spring forth from the back of Iliana, lifting her and Mara higher and higher.

"See! Iliana — a — angel!" Aaron too was looking up, watching as Iliana lifted Mara. "She — got — wings!"

In silence, Luke Johnson, the pilot, and the other rescuers stood with the sheriff and the children, staring into the morning sky as Iliana and Mara slowly lifted from sight. Only Micah remained kneeling, holding the lifeless body of a small child in her arms. Then the sheriff heard again the song that he had heard Aaron sing on the trail as they had made their way to the clearing "Jesus — love — me — this — I — know…"

Peace

The grass in the front yard had greened up from the spring rains. It seemed as though it had rained almost once a week since the previous fall when the tropical storm had hit. Micah sat on a swing on the freshly painted porch, brushing the hair of the young girl in front of her. She watched Luke throw a football toward Ben, arcing it high in the air as Ben tried to position under it.

"Amy Lynn, your hair is so beautiful and long!" Micah took another brush through the back of her hair.

"Thank you, Mrs. Summers." Amy Lynn's large brown eyes watched ahead as Aaron and a spotted dog scrambled after his older brother, now running with a football toward the hackberry tree. Luke Johnson trailed behind the boys, raising his hands signaling a 'touchdown' after Ben made it to the tree.

A trail of dust coming up the long driveway caught Micah's attention. The patrol car pulled up near the house and stopped, and the now familiar large figure slowly pulled himself from the car.

"Good afternoon, Mrs. Summers," The sheriff called out cheerfully, pulling on his hat as he stepped away from the car.

"Good afternoon, Sheriff. What can I do for you?" Micah looked over the top of the car and saw Luke and the boys come jogging toward the house.

"Well, I just brought some papers for you to sign – you know the government, always more paperwork." The sheriff started up the front porch steps holding a large manila envelope.

Micah took the papers from the sheriff's large hand, and slowly read them. She shook her head slowly as she reached for a pen that the sheriff was holding out to her. Micah signed the paper and handed them back to the sheriff just as Luke and the two boys arrived on the porch.

"Good afternoon, Luke. It's good to see you! How are you two boys doing?" The sheriff extended his hand to Luke, and gave the boys a pat on the shoulder. "I just brought some more papers for Mrs. Summers to sign about, you know, last fall and all."

Luke and the sheriff looked over toward Micah, still sitting on the swing. She was staring out into the sky, hair brush still in her hand.

"Micah?" Luke called out. "Everything all right?"

Micah looked back over to Luke and the sheriff, and smiled, pulling the brush back up to Amy Lynn. "Yeah, everything is fine. It's just that, sometimes, things like that paperwork make me remember – to think back to last fall." Micah looked down at Amy Lynn's hair and continued while stroking the brush across her hair. "You know, I still don't really understand it all. Why she came here, why things turned out the way they did. I mean, I believed in angels and all, but I'm still not sure why she came, why Mara isn't here any more…"

"Angel came to help! Iliana came to help save Mara from dying." Aaron spoke quickly now, words running together into a single sentence. He leaned over Ditto, and rubbed his head. "Angel take Mara to heaven."

Micah looked back up into the clouds, watching as one of the clouds appeared to take on wings. She felt the soft breeze on her face, and thought for a moment she could feel the soft kiss of Mara's lips. "I guess so, Aaron. Sometimes it's just hard to believe."